M000016885

YASHAKIDEN
夜叉姫伝
the DEMON PRINCESS
1

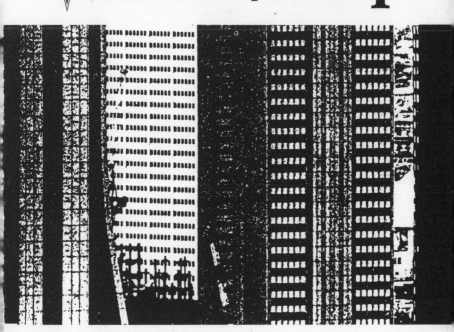

Author's Bio

"Ever since visiting the birthplace of the vampire in Transylvania," Hideyuki Kikuchi recalls, with a gleam in his eye, "the experience has been stoking a desire to write my own vampire novel."

Fans won't be able to tear their eyes away from *Yashakiden*, one of Kikuchi's defining works. In 1985, the highly-anticipated *Makaikou* was published to great acclaim, propelling Kikuchi into bestselling author status like a rocket. Today, his reputation as a versatile "writer-of-all-trades" remains unquestioned among the Japanese reading population.

Hideyuki Kikuchi was born in 1949 in Choshi, Chiba Prefecture. While studying law at Aoyama University, he participated in the college's "mystery and detective novel" club. After graduation, he published stories in *doujinshi* magazines and translated science fiction while working as a magazine reporter.

His debut as a novelist came in 1982 with the publication of *Demon City Shinjuku*.

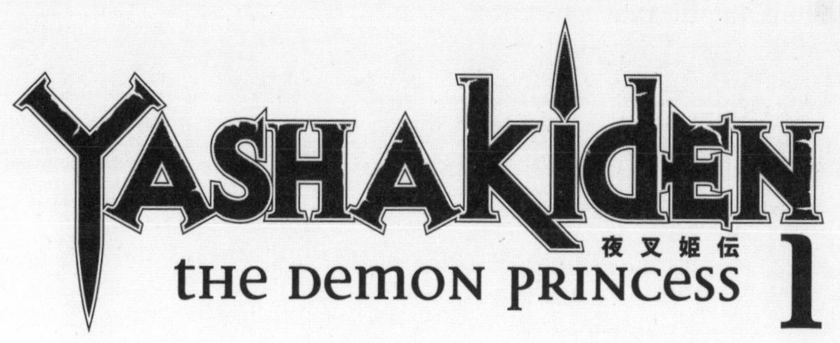

Written by
HIDEYUKI KIKUCHI

Illustrations by
JUN SUEMI

English Translation by
Eugene Woodbury

Los Angeles

Yashakiden: The Demon Princess Vol. 1

Yashakiden:The Demon Princess vol.1 - Yashakiden 1 © Hideyuki Kikuchi 1997. Originally published in Japan in 2007 by SHODENSHA Publishing Co.,LTD. English translation copyright © 2009 by DIGITAL MANGA, Inc. All other material © 2009 by DIGITAL MANGA, Inc. All rights reserved. No portion of this publication may be reproduced or transmitted in any form or by any means without written permission from the copyright holders. Any likeness of characters, places, and situations featured in this publication to actual persons (living or deceased), events, places, and situations are purely coincidental. All characters depicted in sexually explicit scenes in this publication are at least the age of consent or older. The DMP logo is ™ of DIGITAL MANGA, Inc.

Written by Hideyuki Kikuchi
Illustrated by Jun Suemi
English Translation by Eugene Woodbury

English Edition Published by:

DIGITAL MANGA PUBLISHING
A division of DIGITAL MANGA, Inc.
1487 W 178th Street, Suite 300
Gardena, CA 90248
USA
www.dmpbooks.com

Library of Congress Cataloging-in-Publication Data Available Upon Request

First Edition: December 2009
ISBN-13: 978-1-56970-145-4
10 9 8 7 6 5 4 3 2 1

Printed in Canada

YASHAKIDEN
夜叉姫伝
THE DEMON PRINCESS 1

Contents

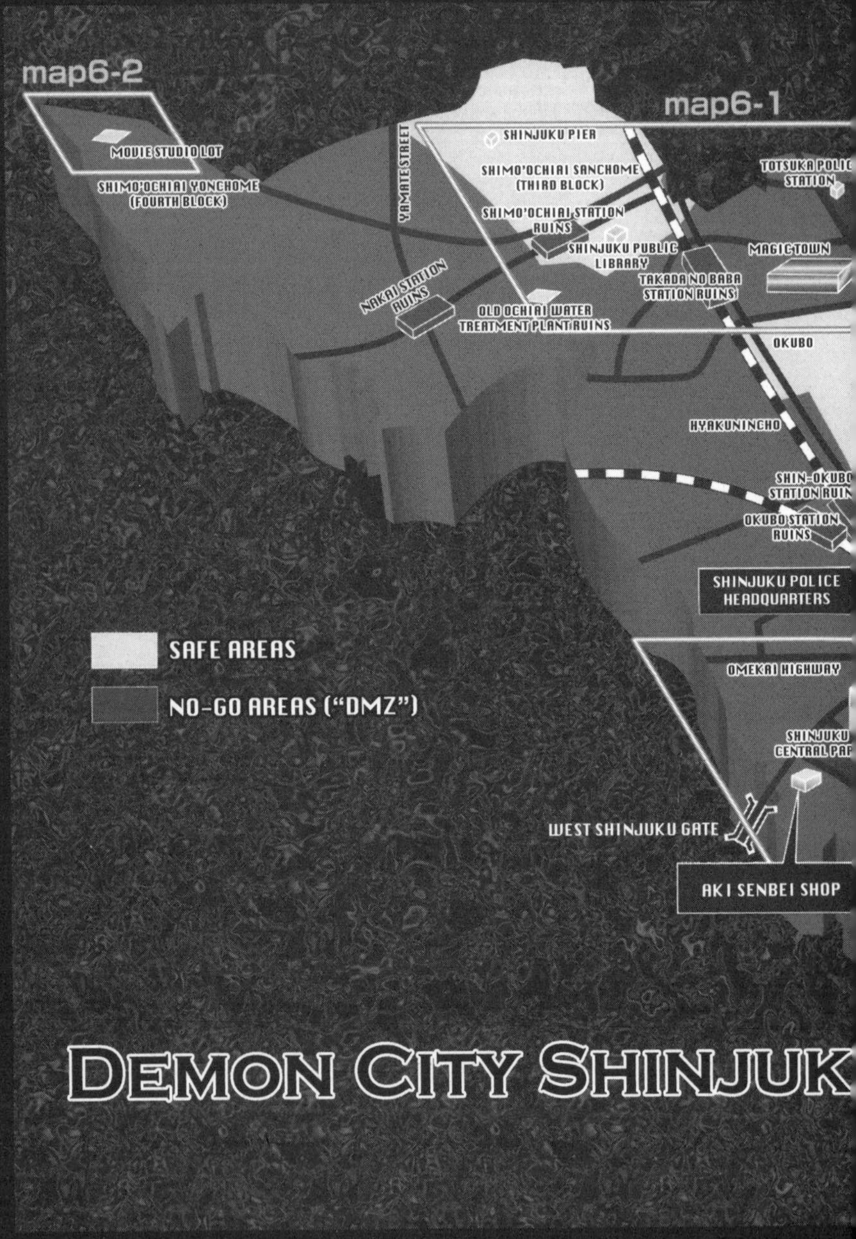

map6-2

map6-1

MOVIE STUDIO LOT

SHIMO'OCHIAI YONCHOME (FOURTH BLOCK)

YAMATE STREET

SHINJUKU PIER

SHIMO'OCHIAI SANCHOME (THIRD BLOCK)

TOTSUKA POLIC STATION

SHIMO'OCHIAI STATION RUINS

SHINJUKU PUBLIC LIBRARY

MAGIC TOWN

TAKADA NO BABA STATION RUINS

NAKAI STATION RUINS

OLD OCHIAI WATER TREATMENT PLANT RUINS

OKUBO

HYAKUNINCHO

SHIN-OKUBO STATION RUIN

OKUBO STATION RUINS

SHINJUKU POLICE HEADQUARTERS

SAFE AREAS

NO-GO AREAS ("DMZ")

OMEKAI HIGHWAY

SHINJUKU CENTRAL PAR

WEST SHINJUKU GATE

AKI SENBEI SHOP

DEMON CITY SHINJUK

WASEDA GATE
map5
YAMABUKICHO
SHIMOMIYABICHO
KAGURAZAKA
WASEDA BOULEVARD
YARAICHO
TAIHEI PHOTOGRAPHY STUDIO
BENTENCHO
SOUTH ENOKICHO
KIKUICHO
HAKONE MOUNTAIN
TOYAMA HOUSING PROJECT
EAST GAIEN STREET
OKUBO AVENUE
ICHIGAYAKAGACHO
WAKAMATSUCHO
JSDF (JAPAN SELF-DEFENSE FORCES) ICHIGAYA GARRISON
KAWADACHO
FUJI TELEVISION RUINS
SHINJUKU AQUARIUM
SHOKUAN AVENUE
POWER STATION
YOCHOMACHI
SUMIYOSHICHO
YASUKUNI AVENUE
KABUKICHO
TOMIHISACHO
NISHIYA GATE
FURIN ASSEMBLY HALL
KOMA THEATER
GOLDEN GAI
PENSION FUND ASSOCIATION BUILDING RUINS
SAN'EICHO
map3
SHINJUKU AVENUE
MEPHISTO HOSPITAL
SHINJUKU NI-CHOME (SECOND BLOCK)
SAMONCHO
SHINJUKU STATION RUINS
SHINJUKU GARDENS
NAITOMACHI
SHINANOMACHI
map2
KEIO UNIVERSITY HOSPITAL RUINS
SHINANOMACHI STATION RUINS
THE KASBAH (BABEL)
MEIJI SHRINE GARDENS
map4
map1

Author's Note

I'm excited to present this novel to the world. Creating a heroic, vampire-themed, supernatural conflict has long been a dream of mine. In these pages, Demon City Shinjuku confronts its greatest enemy. I can't say this is the sole reason, but *Yashakiden* has grown into an epic fantasy series of over a thousand pages.

Ideas bubbled up in my head, and I couldn't bring myself to discard any of them. I sense that what's coming next will exceed anything I imagined. My allegiances to the subject matter have changed along the way. I'm fond of my vampires, breathing new life into them as the haunted air of Demon City Shinjuku becomes its own worst enemy.

This story is why this city exists.

Hideyuki Kikuchi

菊地秀行

Part One:
Ghost Ship

Preface

This will be an attempt to explain the “demon” in Demon City Shinjuku. But there are facets to the city that even the old-timers can’t wrap their heads around.

Starting with human beings, an inorganic city incorporates the organic. It grows, divides, renews itself, and thus achieves a kind of asexual reproduction. Shinjuku similarly remakes itself in a flash, moment by moment revealing to mortal eyes entirely different aspects of itself.

For example: Women’s Fashions on the third floor of the New Isetan Department Store. Ever since its construction, the southwest wall of the third floor has mysteriously expanded and contracted day in and day out, mutating into the shape of the human female pudendum. All the while maintaining its polished finish and the hardness of the stressed concrete beneath.

As a consequence, now only women work and shop there.

A huge department store like Isetan wasn’t about to ban male customers for reasons of architectural modesty. But as soon as men caught sight of the cursed wall, they couldn’t resist curiously drawing nearer and touching it. Medical facilities were located on the third floor, with specialists standing by.

Except that most of the doctors, not to mention the

delivery boys, were men as well.

Entranced by the wall, falling into stupors, their faces contorted in ecstasy, many of the male customers climaxed on the spot. In severe cases they collapsed from sexual exhaustion. According to rumors spread by the shop girls, this was a consequence of them getting randy with the women doctors.

But nobody could really say for certain.

The transformations of the wall continue, and computer simulations predict that in several years it will develop the capabilities of a fully functioning female reproductive tract. Finding this an intolerable prospect, store management is said to be seriously considering taking a jackhammer to the whole thing.

For example: A tree that grows in a corner of Kabuki-cho, one of Demon City's pleasure districts. In this decadent and corrupt city, not a branch is broken and no obscene graffiti mars its trunk. Not only because apples, pears, grapes and persimmons mysteriously appear on its branches day and night, but because everybody knows that anyone who touches it will meet a bad end.

Botanists from outside Shinjuku speculate that the tree is undergoing mutations at the cellular level. But the cause is unclear. Psychics hired by the Shinjuku ward alderman claim that the tree has its own objectives in mind, but they can't say what those are.

For example: The street that goes up the hill from Kagurazaka to Yaraicho. The buildings lining this street change every twenty-four hours like clockwork.

The bookstores, appliance dealers, music shops, restaurants, houses—those wishing to see the transformation of these run-of-the-mill structures must climb the hill at dawn. No other time of day will do. The magic never occurs while descending the hill, either.

The buildings become shrouded like phantoms in a mist. Then overlapping and eclipsing them, as if being born from within, a different row of buildings appears.

Even though none of the visitors who hike the hill work there, they keep coming back. Because at that instant they might catch a glimpse of a lost husband or wife, or child or lover in the row of houses, as if frozen in amber from before the city's violent destruction and resurrection.

But the visitor is just as likely to see the ancient past or vistas from distant lands. White stone buildings in Greece overlooking the vivid blue Mediterranean. Ancient cities of the Gobi Desert shrouded in blowing sand. Eastern European villages surrounded by deep, dark forests.

They appear before the eyes; and disappear with the light of dawn.

Nevertheless, the "demon" in Demon City Shinjuku will not be found there. The incomprehensible nature of these ongoing transfigurations must be accepted for what it is. Shinjuku's demonic nature persists, stubborn and undeterred, and such mysteries serve only to hint at the deeper truths hidden beneath.

And yet, every now and then, as if stepping into the wan glow at the borderline between light and dark, the incomprehensible is made visible. The joy felt in those moments comes from that mysterious thrill in the brain when it solves a puzzle or gains some new insight.

But there is also forbidden fruit that must not be eaten. Things that must not be seen. Even in Demon City.

What occurred on a summer night marks the beginning of one such story.

Chapter One

The night was so steaming hot that just *thinking* about breaking a sweat was enough to break a sweat. People were dropping like flies from dehydration. The street vendors sold everything they had on hand to quench the thirst. Before they knew it, they'd bartered away their own supplies and were collapsing from the heat as well.

It wasn't hard to read a foreboding symbolism into these events.

Rubber-soled shoes stuck to the asphalt and let out a pinched squeal with each step. The ward mayor ordered the sprinkler trucks to raise a curtain of steam. Not because it accomplished anything, but because it put on a good show.

The weather wasn't like this during the day. It had suddenly turned at midnight. As if choreographed.

A pale hand raised a glass. The amber liquid that half-filled it barely stirred. Lips beautiful enough to make even a man shudder at the sight pressed against the transparent rim. The young woman sitting on a barstool several seats away exclaimed in a long, low voice that sounded like a sigh.

Her boyfriend reacted with a fierce glare at the owner of the glass, and then he gaped as he tried to glower. Setsura Aki silently set the empty glass down on the counter.

"You sure can put 'em down," the bartender said with a straight face. He and the customer went way back. "That makes three. I've got five more bottles cooling in the refrigerator."

"Much appreciated," said Setsura, sheepishly brushing the tip of his nose with his forefinger. "But barley tea doesn't make me much of a customer. Not compared to the typical beer drinker."

"Don't give me that. I charge the same for a whiskey and water." The bartender's leathery face split into a boyish grin. "Still, you pull a rabbit out of the hat every time I see you. Here it is the dead of summer, and you're all in black. It's not natural, even assuming you were one for putting on airs. Not a thread out of place."

Setsura laughed with youthful awkwardness.

"You couldn't tell from looking at me, but my mom's a fashion designer in the outside world. When I was a kid, she'd tan my hide if she caught me going goth. *That's not a color that belongs in the real world*, she'd say. It's the same reason people wear black to funerals, trying in their own simple way to stand apart. Black belongs to the other side, suited to the dead and the gods of death. Fits you to a T, Aki-san."

"I'm very much alive. I even cast a shadow."

"But you aren't sweating." The bartender wiped his dripping forehead with a damp towel. "My old air conditioner gives up the ghost on nights like this. I'm soaked all the way down to my drawers. And there you sit in that black duster like it's Antarctica."

"Business hasn't been so good lately." Setsura thumbed the cuff of his right sleeve. "Look, I'm down to my last good suit."

"Still, it's been an awfully quiet night. Strange."

As a rejoinder like *that's for sure* would logically

follow such a statement, Setsura looked up at the bartender in a gesture of agreement.

"The nights are never quiet when it's this hot. Maybe during the day. But when the evening comes, everybody kicks back under the trees in the shade of the buildings, and the street musicians and the soapbox preachers entertain them. None of that at all tonight."

"At all?" Setsura echoed.

The bartender caught his breath, suddenly drawn into the ominous, endless depths of those enchanting eyes. No—it was only his imagination. There was some vast, calming force adrift in that penetrating gaze. That was all. The same as always.

"Nothing," said the bartender, smoothing over the moment with a smile.

Setsura said shortly, "It's like a funeral."

"Eh?"

"Or the exact opposite."

The bartender didn't have a comeback for that.

"Death is the second life. I read that in a Chinese book somewhere."

"It's from the *Sankoshou,*" said the young woman on the barstool. She'd been studiously ignoring her boyfriend while eavesdropping on the conversation between Setsura and the bartender. "A book of aphorisms compiled by Shu Yuan during the Tang Dynasty. '*Death gives birth to the second life. And so we wait, our heads bowed, defeated in spirit, waiting as if for the mighty emperor and empress to appear.*' "

"Indeed—" Setsura turned and smiled at her.

The flash of his brilliant white teeth alone was enough to make her press her hand against her ample chest.

"Hey, get a grip," said the boyfriend in obvious

consternation, shaking her shoulder.

"I'm sorry. I just can't. I've never seen a man so fine before. God, I love this place." She hung her head.

"I told you," the bartender said to the boyfriend with a knowing smile. "You probably don't want to hear it from me, but it's not his fault. You were trying too hard to close the deal. Three vodkas are too much for any woman."

"Maybe you should call a cab then." Though he had a round face, the girl's boyfriend was handsome in his own way. He both precisely articulated and rushed his words at the same time.

"Sure thing," the bartender said, the smile staying on his face. He reached for the cordless phone nearby. The number of the cab company was a single button push away.

As the bartender brought the phone to his mouth, Setsura mumbled something to himself. He always had an air about him of having just crawled out of bed. But now he said, for no particular reason, in a deadly serious tone of voice that raised the hairs on the bartender's arms, *"Our heads bowed, defeated in spirit, we wait for the mighty emperor and empress to appear.* This is that kind of night."

The bartender didn't answer. Instead, he stared at the dark scene beyond the reinforced glass windows behind Setsura. "Shinjuku Taxi," he heard on the other end of the line.

The moon was rising. It was a night so beautiful he could imagine hearing the music of the heavenly spheres. Not a cloud in the sky. Instead of clouds, long shadows darker than the transparent night struggled for a place in the empty air.

Some shadows reached straight and tall. Others

slanted against the horizon. During the day, the countless fissures running along the walls plainly pointed to a future time when a grotesque tragedy would befall Shinjuku.

The once glass-smooth roads held the scars of terrible cracks and fractures. On starlit nights, the wind whistling through the trees seemed to be singing a funeral dirge.

Everybody knew it wouldn't be long before the soaring, chalk-white buildings at the center of political activity in the new city would be lying beneath the brilliant moonlight like broken sepulchres. The word *old* had already been attached to Shinjuku City Hall and the forest of high-rises surrounding it.

To the west was Chuo Park, Shinjuku's DMZ. The skyscraper district was a no-go area surrounded by chain-link fences and razor wire. But the view of the moon was just as beautiful no matter where it was observed on the planet.

But perhaps—because the foreboding air that enshrouded the city drove the boorish obstructions of the sky from the senses—whether a new or full moon, the lunar orb took on a brilliant glow as if lit from within. On most nights, the shadows falling here and there on the streets would be cast instead by photographers transfixed by its beauty.

And with guides and bodyguards at the ready, the relatively safer grounds of the Park Hyatt and Hilton Tokyo housed an even larger crowd of artists, poets and writers.

This night though, the whirlpools of heat had the artistic spirits on the run. The only shadows were cast by trees lining the roadways. And at the northern border of the skyscraper district, the all-night bar on the corner facing Fifth Street—normally busy with admirers of the moon—was dead as a doornail.

"The moon's almost too bright tonight," said the bartender. The taxi company he'd dialed had at some point hung up.

In this city, something *too* beautiful was cause for suspicion. The bartender glanced at Setsura, but not in expectation of a reply. The exquisite young man had his eyes closed.

Setsura then opened his eyes. Looking down into his barley tea he said, "There was a river."

"Huh?" The bartender knitted his brows. He'd heard him distinctly, but the words made no sense. This city was stocked to the gills with the bizarre and the unnatural, but it did not have a river.

The bartender had settled in Shinjuku just five years before. But those words would have struck fear through the hearts of the old-timers who knew the place before the "Devil Quake."

There was no swift-flowing river. But there was a river—a river entirely appropriate to this city. Setsura again closed his eyes. Invisible colors were visible to this beautiful, haunted man. Unheard sounds were audible to his ears.

"You can't hear it?" His voice almost sang the question.

"Nope." The bartender shook his head. He looked out the window at Fifth Street. At the glittering white light pouring down.

It was—*water.*

"What the hell!?" The drunken girl's boyfriend cried out.

This wasn't an apparition created by the dazzling moon. The glittering silver current coursing down the concrete surface of the road was the real thing.

A young woman was singing the blues. A fair-skinned lass in a black dress, only in her twenties, but the timbre of her voice was as full and rich as it was relaxed and unforced. When she sang the blues it swept the regulars away to a different place.

As if a youngster like that could sing!

And yet the songs of this "youngster" impressed professional singers to tears, while tough-skinned veteran performers grieved in private knowing they'd never be her equal.

That was the power of the blues. It was said of this girl on stage that the blues had chosen *her*.

The applause swelled as the reverberations of the final stanza drifted through the dimly-lit room. Not a single boorish catcall or cheer.

"Man, she's got a set of pipes!" The man spoke passionately, rubbing his palms together. He took a deep breath and exhaled. "What do you think, Doctor? Good as any *out there*. Word is, she's been singing here for five years, absorbing the mood of this city into her music. I gotta say, this is one helluva town."

He looked for a sign of agreement from his guest seated across the table. He received none.

"I guess if the good Doctor wanted something better, he could manufacture a perfect pair of vocal cords himself." His intention was to enliven the mood, but he paled as soon as he spoke, hearing the mocking tone in his words.

"Perhaps we shall listen to something else for the time being."

A voice like deep water spilling over polished gems.

A voice that made the two scantily-clad hostesses on either side of him catch their breath.

Had the voice belonged to a statue, then its sculptor must have given up his soul to carve something so beautiful. A corner of his white cape was draped over his right hand, which contained all the powers of the demon world. It was said that he could cure any disease with nothing more than a rusty knife.

A physical beauty that caused, from a single glance, a paralyzing sense of emptiness akin to death. That was why he was called "Doctor Mephisto."

The Demon Physician.

"What do you mean by that, Doctor? You don't want to listen to the blues anymore?"

"I'm not really sure myself," the Doctor answered this time.

"Huh," the man responded in confusion. His attention turned to the brandy snifter sitting in front of Mephisto. "Hey, what's going on?" he shouted. "His glass isn't topped off!"

The hostesses flanking the Doctor normally would have attended to the task. Neither of them moved a muscle. As soon as they'd sat down next to the electrifyingly attractive doctor, the two had fallen under the spell of his indescribable unearthly presence.

"That's fine," Mephisto said softly. "Drinking isn't my *forte*."

"Oh, come on," the man said, waving his hand dismissively.

Three empty bottles of cognac were lined up on the table. The best spirits from the outside world. They were rare as hen's teeth in Demon City, costing a good five hundred thousand yen apiece. Mephisto's handiwork, downing what he'd been offered.

Marveling to himself, the man produced a new bottle. "Bottoms up, Doctor."

Mephisto didn't refuse. He raised the empty glass to receive the smoky golden liquid, and then downed it in a single gulp. Without taking a breath or wiping his mouth. Not leaving a single drop behind. Almost as if the alcohol had sprung into his mouth of its own accord.

"That's one hollow leg you have," the man said with honest admiration. "Your cheeks aren't even flushed. Incredible! Doctor, I'm telling you, when the time for hospital expansion comes, just give me a shout. I may not look it, but I can get my hands on unlisted properties that never show up on the market."

He wasn't lying. A real estate broker who'd made Shinjuku his home turf, his Kabuki-cho offices had a hand stirring every pot in the ward, from the grubbiest shack to the coveted ruins of the Self-Defense Forces buildings.

His wife had been stricken by a malignant tumor. After his personal doctor and shamans declared her condition hopeless and threw in the towel, he'd brought her to Mephisto's hospital. Mephisto cured her in ten seconds. The little party he was throwing tonight was his way of expressing his gratitude.

"Say, Doctor, girls aren't your thing?"

The man cast a quick glance at the cordon of women surrounding them. The best nightclub in Kabuki-cho, stocked with the prettiest women money could buy, and none of them were getting the job done. Tell one to pour a drink, and it'd go all over the table. Crack a joke, and they'd just sit there and stare into space.

The man had kept his temper in check only because he knew they were acting that way because of Mephisto.

Maybe they were intimidated by his looks, or some other obstacle prevented them from getting up close and friendly. As much as he needled, pushed and shoved, they wouldn't press any closer. But they didn't stand up and walk away either. They just sat and stared at him like beings possessed. It made the man shiver.

"You like women?" Mephisto asked.

"Of course!" From his wife down to a college coed, the man had four lovers.

"To me, everyone is the same. I feel that way especially after an operation."

"You do have a point there."

"If the insides are the same, all that's left to choose from is the outward appearance. Do you understand what I'm getting at?"

"Yeah, sure."

"When there is no need to willingly choose that which is ugly, then *this* is what remains."

Mephisto lightly stroked his cheek with his left forefinger. When he did it, it didn't seem off-putting at all. No one would disagree with his assessment.

"That means that—guy or girl—you're fine with them as long as they're pretty? Not to be crude, but you're saying you play for both teams?"

The man flashed a smile, then froze. The eyes of the women flanking Mephisto rolled back. The taut unearthly aura flowing around Mephisto suddenly snapped.

"D-Doctor—"

The room fell silent. The man's eyes focused on Mephisto's face, which shone with a brilliant white light in the darkened room.

"Pretty?" he probed. "Has the human race devised a more miserable standard of description? Are you incapable of imagining the existence of a beauty that you yourself remain unaware of? Have you not ever felt that way? Such stale adjectives are suited only for those who know nothing of vistas that the stunted human brain cannot fathom."

From far away, applause beat against the man's eardrums. The singer was mounting the stage again.

"Nevertheless, the female sex is undeniably an object of enormous fascination. You could even call it an imperative—from a doctor's perspective."

Mephisto gracefully opened his arms and wrapped them around the hostesses at either side. At the same time, as if escaping the ghostly spell, the dazed expression on the man's face returned to normal. But his eyes still stared.

Mephisto's fingers slowly crawled across a white shoulder. *Ahh!* the woman gasped.

"Fair skin, a generous distribution of fat, internal organs in good health—nevertheless, unawares, without lifting a finger, they will rot away beneath spotted, aging skin—the epitome of transience."

Mephisto's hand reached the woman's breast that was pushing out of the top of her dress, a dress slit far up the thigh. The man gaped as Mephisto's fingers sank into the soft, white flesh without denting or creasing the skin, like a craftsman driving in a nail.

"What a waste," said Mephisto with complete sincerity. "An utter waste. Mothers who have reared their children and women who will never give birth—to them, what good are these but to tempt men? They need simply say the word and—*gone.* And given in exchange, a meaningful and purposeful life worth living."

"A bit over the top, aren't you, Doc? They're just boobs."

The mood in the nightclub abruptly changed. A noisy rustle rose from one end to the other.

"What's that voice saying?"

"No, what's that *sound*?"

The audience commotion drew the man's attention toward the stage. Mephisto stared intently at his glass. A small, strange tragedy was about to be born.

The singer pressed her hands against her throat. Gasping, unable to breathe, the air squeaked out of her lungs in an asthmatic scream. She writhed, her mouth open, a hoarse cry drawn out of her body like a thin thread. Finally the sound welled up and spilled out.

Zaa— Zaa— Zaa— Zaa—

The sound caused more confusion than terror. A sound nobody had ever heard before.

Zaa— Zaa— Zaa— Zaa—

The sound of onrushing water.

From the lips of this blues singer, said to be second in talent only to Shinobu Kaze, poured a sparkling sweet sound, like a melody played on a koto. A gorgeous timbre. A sad song. And an expression of unmitigated joy.

The audience forgot the extraordinary sight of the bewitched performer and sank into a collective trance.

"*Come*," said a man's voice.

And in that instant, the singer cried out.

A silver shaft as wide as her mouth sprang from her throat and smashed into the audience, scattering screaming patrons and sending a shower of splinters flying in all directions.

A column of bone-chilling cold water.

The white shadow made its way like a phantom through the fleeing customers. Everybody knew the exquisite young man cloaked in the pure white cape, but the purpose of the brandy snifter peeking out from the seams of the cloak was a mystery.

The singer bent backward, and then pitched forward. The water arced forth from the depths of the sea and channeled through her throat. It didn't touch the floor.

Doctor Mephisto stood directly in front of the onrushing waters.

The night's incident was destined to become one more curious case in the medical files of the Demon Physician. Even before that, the story would take on a life of its own, another chapter in "the legend of Doctor Mephisto."

Every drop of water gushing from the singer's lips was sucked into the glass Mephisto held in his hand.

Chapter Two

Zaa— Zaa— Zaa— Zaa—

The sound coursed along Fifth Street.

"What the hell is going on?" the bartender wondered. He stood on the stoop and peered at the waters swirling beneath the steps.

"The taxi!" the boyfriend wailed. "Where's my taxi!"

"Button it," said Setsura Aki. The reverberations made him think of winter frost. The bar was wrapped in silence. "Can't you hear it?" Setsura pressed. "Can't you?"

"Not at all," the bartender answered.

"Not at all," the boyfriend echoed.

"I can."

Setsura slid off the stool. He went to the window and slid it open. The expected wave of heat did not sweep through the opening. Instead, he breathed out white mist. He could see his breath. When the road became a flowing river, the heat had turned to a bone-chilling cold.

"*All will bow their heads and wait*," Setsura intoned, staring intently at the rushing waters before his eyes. "Even the heat. Obviously somebody is putting on a production. But who is directing the play?"

Born in fire to reign in ice. And somebody was arranging a coronation ceremony behind the scenes.

The bartender craned his head. "I hear it," he said in a small voice.

"I hear it," the boyfriend said.

From the far reaches of the river in the direction of the Hilton Tokyo, a sweet and painful melody accompanied the eerily approaching world that flowed towards them.

The sound of a koto.

"*They're coming*," Setsura Aki said. "Just like in the legends."

At the same moment, he couldn't have known that those same words were being repeated in the corner of a nightclub in Kabuki-cho.

The sound drew closer. And something else as well. The bartender began to shiver, and it wasn't just because of the cold.

Setsura saw it first, emerging from the depths of the darkness. A black ship glided toward them. The oddly raised bow of the boat appeared first. Two masts. The sails were furled. An old and weathered hull.

Not steel. A wooden ship, not one from this era. Ten oar holes dotted the hull at the waterline. Wooden sculls stuck out of the holes, hovering horizontally over the surface of the water.

"There are people there," Setsura heard the bartender say behind him.

The silhouettes of three people on the deck. Three people who looked back at them.

On the left was an old man with white hair and beard, thin as a crane. Next to him was a girl. She still had youth left in her. Her luxurious black hair was tied up in buns behind each ear. Her large eyes flitted about her surroundings, taking it all in.

The third person had a young and graceful countenance. Between his full eyebrows was a small dot, like an embedded pearl. All of them were decked out in Chinese clothing gorgeously woven with threads of silver and gold. All their eyes focused on Setsura.

The girl disappeared. She'd left to fetch somebody.

The sound of the koto ceased.

The girl returned with a new person. It was as if a halo of light had blossomed between the girl and the old man. That was how radiantly attractive this new woman was. On a par with Setsura, with Doctor Mephisto even.

Her black hair fluttered gently to one side in the wind, casting a shadow across her snow-white skin and white robes. Standards of beauty changed with the years, with the eras, and from country to country. But the beauty of this woman—no older than twenty—was eternal and immutable, surpassing every possible expectation.

The sound of the koto rang out. Setsura couldn't see her hands, but they must have been playing the music.

Their eyes met for several long seconds. The ship crossed from right to left, from the heart of darkness toward the heart of Shinjuku, where some rough beast was waiting to be born.

Setsura silently watched as the ship slowly slipped by.

The koto sounded again. A voice like a silver bell began to recite a poem. Setsura translated the ancient language in his head.

Crossing the waters we've crossed before
Seeing the flowers we've seen once more
Spring breezes along the riverbank roads
Before we know it, we've made our way home

The verses wafted through the frozen night air, evaporating as they reached his ears. These four strangers were right now sailing to Shinjuku.

Setsura looked at the quiet moon high in the night sky.

"That's a nice smell," the bartender mumbled to himself. "Perfume? From what country?" He wiped his face with his hands.

Setsura noticed it as well. The heat was making a comeback.

"The water's retreating," the bartender observed.

Without a second glance at the sparkling wet pavement, Setsura shut the window and returned to the counter.

"What happened just now?" the bartender asked. "It's like being inside a living dream. That happens a lot around here, you know."

"Maybe so," Setsura said, grasping his glass of tea. "But there are dreams we're better off not seeing. Dreams that should not become real." He drained the remainder of the tea.

The boyfriend cried out, almost on the verge of tears, "Hey, hey, where's the taxi?"

Michio Hyuuga couldn't settle down. The sense of unease carved a hole in the pit of his stomach. Combined with the tightness around his ankles, it made his insides feel like a loose sock full of rocks. He had no idea why. He cursed and swore, but venting didn't do him any good. All he could do was throw up his hands in exasperation.

He wanted to talk it over with somebody. He had—albeit vaguely—a candidate in mind. A real egghead. A straight dealer with a well-established reputation. And having real muscle at his disposal couldn't hurt. The problem was, for an ordinary working stiff, getting in good with a guy like that was way out of his league.

But nothing ventured, nothing gained. Hyuuga was in agony. The sweet music strummed in his ears. *A guitar*, he thought.

He looked around. Grubby little shops, with doors and windows shuttered. He seemed to have wandered down a back alleyway. No streetlights, but the moon shone brightly overhead. His shadow was clearly outlined at his feet.

In front of him, another shadow approached. Hyuuga raised his head and started a bit.

A young girl dressed in a *cheongsam* bowed to him, her sleeved hands clasped in front of her chest. She smiled. In the dark, her crimson lips took on an adorable hue.

Hyuuga shook his intoxicated head and thought through the situation. He was on a Kabuki-cho side street. Though the main thoroughfares were relatively safe, the back alleys required a lot more diligence. Especially at this hour.

He wasn't particularly worried about stumbling across the odd cat-eyed snake or man-eating rat. The regular "monster eradication campaign" had swept through the Kabuki-cho district two days ago with poison gas and flame throwers, and that generally kept the critters out for the better part of a week. Besides, today was his day off, and he owed himself a drink or two.

The girl was either a pickpocket or a prostitute. He didn't have much cash on him and wasn't in the mood anyway. So either option was a non-starter.

"What'cha want, little lady?" Hyuuga asked, trying to keep it polite.

She didn't answer, smiled sweetly again, and then casually leapt into the air. She didn't even crouch and jump. Hyuuga automatically craned his head back and felt the hairs rise on the back of his neck.

"Hey, you—" he said.

A pale hand appeared to the right side of his face. The forefinger pointed forward.

"What are you doing—?" He didn't finish the question. He gaped in astonishment. He was walking, and not of his own accord. "H-Hold on a second. Hey—you—"

The finger before his terror-stricken eyes flexed at the knuckles, now pointing to the left. He noticed the black maw of an alley opening like a mouth. He was turning into it.

When the silhouette emerged from the side street and walked towards her, Hisako Tokoyoda nonchalantly pointed her handbag in its direction.

She'd found the "armored handbag" at the Hanazono Shrine discount bazaar. It turned out to have more capabilities than its price suggested, and Hisako was delighted with her find.

The handbag held a .25 caliber Colt pocket auto with an eight-round magazine. The safety release and trigger were operated by a single lever. Plenty of capacity and not too bulky. These days, bullets of that caliber made for self-defense were mostly high-velocity explosive rounds. At short distances, one would drop a sumo wrestler.

The muzzle jutted through a slit in one end of the handbag. Hisako pointed it at the approaching figure, proud of her ability to keep her cool.

She still wasn't over the shock of getting assaulted by magical forces earlier that evening at the nightclub. But she should come out of it unscathed. In any case, she'd take a sick day, drop by the hospital tomorrow, and everything would soon return to normal.

Besides, this was the 2nd block bus stop in Kabuki-cho. The bus would be by soon. No place was truly safe after hours, so the ward government ran old retrofitted surface-street buses until morning in order to accommodate the drunks and graveyard shift workers. Passes were cheap and for sale everywhere.

Three yards away, and the man showed no signs of stopping. Hisako flipped the lever to the right. The safety released with a soft *click*. A round was already chambered. One more twist and this loaded gun would go off.

"What do you want?" she asked.

He didn't answer.

She felt the numb tenseness seeping into her left hand at about the same time the man came to a halt. He stopped beneath the glow of a streetlight. Seeing his face, Hisako felt her apprehension begin to dissolve. His noble, graceful countenance was enough to prompt her to let go of that dangerous lever.

Despite the heat of the night, he was wearing a dark cloak with the collar turned up. It looked Chinese.

At any rate, though, this was a fine-looking man.

"You here for the bus as well?" Hisako asked, the tension disappearing from her voice.

"I am not," the young man replied, in hesitant Japanese.

So he must be Chinese. Anybody from anywhere could be found in this town.

"Then what are you doing here?" she probed, her voice tightening again.

"There is something I want. Here."

Despite the radiant smile on his face, Hisako again pressed her finger against the trigger. "Well, sorry, but you can take a hike. I've got nothing for you."

"No." The young man slowly shook his head. "Everyone has what I want. You are overflowing with it inside."

"Well, aren't you a bad boy. Seriously, I'm into hot guys as much as the next girl. But if you don't take it elsewhere and quick, I'm gonna have to shoot you."

"Shoot?"

"Yeah. Like, *bang, bang*. You see this?" Hisako held up the bag and pointed with her right hand at the gun.

The young man shrugged, and continued to advance.

"I said, *freeze*!"

Only three feet between them now. The bag shook and spat fire. A black dot, blacker than the cloak he was wearing, appeared in the center of the man's chest. A dull, rending sound came from inside his body. He reached out his hand. The smile on his face didn't fade. *Just a little fun between lovers*, said the look in his eyes.

"Stop!" Hisako cried.

Her finger repeatedly squeezed the trigger.

The shots came one after the other.

The young man was standing right in front of her. She couldn't miss. His sturdy frame bent slightly backwards with the impact of each bullet, and shook from the explosions that followed. But that was all.

He took hold of Hisako's shoulders. His fingers dug into skin. Hisako screamed, more in terror than in pain. She'd begun to grasp that he wouldn't be any more forgiving because of her gender. He would tear a child limb from limb if it suited him.

Before she could scream again, he pulled her against his chest. She saw that his lips, black in the light of the streetlamp, were so red they almost glowed.

"We have just completed a long sea voyage. We are hungry. You look delicious."

Stop—Hisako whimpered, but couldn't articulate the desire.

The young man bared his teeth. Seeing those ivory spikes, Hisako knew what his true nature was.

Chapter Three

Mephisto called Setsura early the next morning. "Get over here," he said bluntly. "There's something I have to show you."

"The only thing I want to see right now is a good shipment of medium-grain rice," Setsura shot back with equal brusqueness.

"You're a funny man."

"Much appreciated."

"But get your butt over here."

"Wages at that hospital of yours causing employee relations problems? Count me out as a strikebreaker."

"Your occupational skills are of no use to me." Word by word, the unwavering tone of Mephisto's voice ate away at the will of his listener. Such was to be expected of the Demon Physician. "I'm more interested in your moonlighting expertise."

"I have a policy of not accepting jobs from you. Not after what happened the last time."

"That was—" Mephisto didn't finish the sentence. The story was too painful to start dredging up the details. "I thought you were over that."

"I'm carrying it with me to the grave. Now, if you wouldn't mind—"

Setsura waited to hear the long sigh on the other end of the line, before unceremoniously hanging up.

Nevertheless, he arrived at the hospital twenty

minutes later. A nurse was waiting for him in the lobby. She gave him the room number: B401. The first room on the fourth basement level.

"Huh," said Setsura. The special containment ward for hardcore cases. "What's the patient in for?"

"Doctor Mephisto said it was for your eyes only."

"Bastard. No, sorry."

He nodded, and wended his way through the lobby—already packed with patients—to the elevators. He descended nonstop to the fourth underground level. When the elevator doors opened, he was welcomed by a sterile white hallway lit in cold, artificial light.

Hidden from view, every advanced model of sensor, ultrasound paralyzer guns, and lasers made escape impossible.

Some of the patients confined in the underground levels of Mephisto Hospital could take apart an M1 Abrams tank with their bare hands. The walls and floor were reinforced enough to withstand a direct hit from a small nuclear bomb.

Setsura greeted the nurses and guards manning the station in front of the elevators. He stood in front of the door to room B401. The door opened from the inside. It was three times thicker than an ordinary hospital room door. If necessary, it could be electrically charged or emit debilitating gas.

The room itself was quite ordinary. A bed and a spare amount of furniture. Perfectly quiet. On the bed was a young woman in a hospital gown. Setsura leaned back against the door. All he could tell about her was that she was very thin.

Standing at the head of the bed, Mephisto greeted Setsura with a small smile.

Any patient Doctor Mephisto was treating himself

must be handled with all due caution.

"What's up?" Setsura asked, looking again at the woman's emaciated back.

"A police patrol picked her up this morning. Since then she's progressed to a point where nothing seems to be getting through at all. It's not an act."

"Post-traumatic shock, you mean?"

"Not just that."

"You called me first thing in the morning just to string me along?"

Mephisto ignored the retort. "Watch this."

He motioned with his right hand. Light from the ceiling fell vertically onto her head. Despite being on the fourth basement level, it was a shaft of natural sunlight. The woman got up and frailly moved to the left and then sat down on the bed, outside the halo of light.

Setsura asked, "Who is she?"

"Hisako Tokoyoda, according to the I.D. in her handbag. Twenty-seven. She's a singer. We met last night."

"You're branching out."

Mephisto cleared his throat.

"I accepted an invitation. The next morning, she turns up like this. Though something just as strange happened before that."

"Really."

Mephisto went on to describe what had taken place at the nightclub.

Setsura listened without interruption, and then told him about Fifth Street turning into a river, and the ship that sailed past on it.

"Ah. And this girl. Her body must somehow be tuned to their psychic frequency, like a sympathetic vibration. Where do you think they came from?"

"Beyond Shinjuku," was Setsura's immediate response.

Mephisto smiled thinly. "And that would be—*there*?"

Setsura's reply came in the form of a pained look in his eyes. Mephisto nodded. He approached the bed and put his hands on the woman's shoulders, turning her to face Setsura.

Hisako Tokoyoda's face looked like she'd been worked over by a headshrinker, skin stretched tightly around a bleached skull. Blank eyes stared out from sunken sockets. Setsura saw what Mephisto wanted him to see. A pair of fangs protruded from between her waxy lips. On her neck was an ominous pair of scars, like a brand left behind by a hot iron.

"A vampire," said Mephisto, calmly delivering his prognosis.

"A vampire." Setsura blandly repeated.

Neither alarm nor surprise showed on the face of this young owner of a long-established Shinjuku business concern. In this city, such words were hardly unexpected. After all, this was Demon City.

"Have our friends in the Toyama housing project broken their pact?"

Mephisto didn't respond with a yes or no. He stood in front of the woman and thrust his right hand toward her drooping, skeletal head. Her listless black eyes reflected the color of gold. A cross.

At some point, Mephisto had palmed a small crucifix. But she didn't recoil in the slightest, living proof that repudiated the legend. Mephisto briefly pressed the crucifix against her forehead. Not a mark was left on the woman's parchment-like skin.

Setsura observed casually, "Display a cross and

she doesn't recoil in fear. Touch the skin and it doesn't burn. The vampire that bit this woman was certainly not of Western origins. Some of the Toyama residents are made-in-Japan vampires. It's possible that one of them got tired of the artificial stuff and took a little stroll. I should poke around and see what turns up."

Mephisto returned his right hand to the inside of his cape and slowly turned to Setsura. Then, with the same hand he swept up the cape, like a gunfighter flicking back the slicker from his holster. A thin, long glitter of light like a crescent moon. Setsura didn't have time to retreat before Mephisto plunged the elegant blade into his heart.

The handsome *senbei* shop owner grimaced.

Mephisto's arm and the knife did not slacken in their speed, slashing arcs like a swinging pendulum through his body. The moving outlines of the hand and blade disappeared into a blur.

"Damn. Did it again," Mephisto said in a steely voice, replacing his right hand inside his cape. "That happens down here on the fourth level sometimes. I attribute it to the *qi* of the patients. Are you hurt anywhere?"

"I think my heart stopped when you started poking me." Setsura touched the place where the psychic knife had stabbed him. He held up his left palm for Mephisto to see.

Seeing the faint gleam of blood drops on the skin, the Demon Physician sighed heavily.

"Yeah, like deep down you haven't always wanted to do that. Well, no harm, no foul, so I won't hold it against you. Still, this is one freaking spooky hospital you've got."

"I'm grateful to you for grasping that fact. And I'm grateful you didn't garrote me with those filaments of yours. Just to be careful, I should examine your chest later."

"I'll take a rain check. Bake *senbei* too long and the difference between the ideal and the real gets a bit too obvious. So what did you have on your mind?"

"Do you think the scars on this young woman's neck are a result of the hypothetical you suggested?"

"Not really," Setsura readily admitted, withdrawing his previous remarks. "Considering the tight leash they keep on everybody over there, I can't see them breaking the pact come hell or high water. I'm leaning more towards the gang of four I saw the other day."

"Why didn't you just say so in the first place?" Mephisto wondered aloud.

This vampire business had occurred at the same time the phantom river brought those two men and two women to Demon City. And when the nightclub singer had spewed out water. The connection was obvious.

"The woman on the boat was a babe."

Mephisto was dismissive. "Meaning the particular shape and arrangement of nose, eyes and mouth that together you call *beauty*? Who wants to see the *you* in you that isn't *you*?"

"I'll leave this girl to you and check up on those four. That makes you the client. When it comes to the fee, I'll make all due allowances."

Setsura coolly turned around. Behind him, Mephisto said, "The least effort yields the greatest reward."

Setsura glanced over his shoulder. "Meaning?"

"Oh, no, I wouldn't want to detain you any longer."

"Give it a break."

"This girl still hasn't completely turned into a

vampire. The one thing vampires everywhere have in common is that it is never over till the fat lady sings. They will keep on coming until the prey is added to the brood."

"You waiting?" Setsura turned his gaze to the woman sitting on the sheets. He said to Mephisto, "You okay with deliberately drawing the cause of this sickness in here?"

"In cases when a course of treatment cannot be settled upon, exceptions can be made. We'll move her to the general admittance wing of the hospital."

"My, my. What a fine man your doctor is." Setsura shrugged. A grave expression rose on his face. "Assuming those four are at the heart of the matter, this would be the first time we've ever faced down Chinese vampires. I wonder whether comparisons with the Toyama clans are even useful. Can't a clue or two more be gained from her?"

Their eyes met. The woman sat there silently.

"Various investigations are already underway. More precise data based on comparisons with the Toyama residents is coming to light."

"How about that."

"The quantity of blood loss is around 600 cc. Two-and-a-half cups. Twice the 330 cc that the typical Toyama vampire requires. This is only my opinion, but that is more than is necessary to sustain life, so simple starvation must be the cause."

"In that case, why not drain them dead?" Setsura wondered. "It'd save the time and bother of going out every night to visit the victim. There are vamps like that in America."

"The Konsheau incident in Chicago," Mephisto answered at once. He was familiar with cases of the supernatural from around the world. Such was to be expected of the Demon Physician.

Setsura nodded.

Mephisto said, playing the part of the professor lecturing the student, "A Turkish immigrant going by the name of Ray Konsheau. His vampiric nature awakened out of the blue, and from February of 1962 to March of the next year he took the blood of five women. All of them were drained on the spot. Four were buried, but they were delayed in discovering a 37-year-old vagrant by the same of Suzanna Pardue, who turned into a vampire. She attacked four people on the street, until the Special Investigations Unit of the Chicago police drove a stake through her heart. The importance of Konsheau's overnight conversion to a vampiric state was such that after being arrested by the SIU, he was confined to a secret medical facility. His buried victims were disinterred at noon and staked as well."

"The same with Pardue's victims, I assume."

"They'd all been bitten but once. If they'd turned into vampires, that would have been their fate. But according to the SIU's classified report, once Pardue was staked, her victims all returned to normal. The problem is, not knowing the cause, we do not know if what applied in the Konsheau case applies here. This is definitely out of the norm. The possibilities are not pleasant."

A look of undisguised disgust flitted across an icy countenance that would cow anyone who looked upon it. There were reasons for this reaction. The absence of this obsession with the prey—what could be called the vampire's "aesthetic"—was unforgivably *déclassé.*

Why did vampires risk exposure by visiting their victims over and over? Because having been human beings once, and then becoming attached to this dark world, they took pleasure in the *watching*.

As the shadowy secretions contaminated it, the blood maintaining the pink cheeks of the victims turned from red to gray. The skin turned waxy and transparent. In rare cases the blood vessels appeared like coral formations beneath clear water.

The lips lost that spark of life as night by night their incisors grew longer. Eyes became vacant holes gleaming with a devilish fire. The shadows painting their faces gradually darkened. Finally, the victim would die and be reborn in the world of the living dead.

In lengthy cases, when the transformation occurred over a span of several months, the rarity of the species and their relative isolation might explain the happiness they took from slowly digesting all of these tiny details.

But regardless of the age, sex and attractiveness of the victim who'd satisfied their hunger for blood, they approached each visit with the same passion that an artist had for the work of art created by his own hand. Hence the "aesthetic" of the vampire.

Setsura was familiar with this behavior. "Is it so obvious that art should win out over hunger? I think you're talking about the typical vampire. If we sit down with the Toyama bosses, we might be able to come up with some countermeasures."

"You really think so?"

"I do not." Setsura answered at once. A formidable aspect of this handsome young man was emerging from the cocoon, one that brooked no fools or half-measures.

Mephisto permitted himself a small smile.

Setsura stared up at the ceiling. He narrowed his eyes and thought back. "That night, watching the ship sail past before my eyes, I swear the hair stood up on the back of my neck. Those four definitely do not belong here."

He spoke in the same matter-of-fact voice that he always did. But the look on Mephisto's face shifted, tinged with—delight. Even the girl on the bed turned her dumbfounded gaze upon him.

"I will understand once we meet," the transformed Setsura continued. "Human language hides more truths than it reveals. But what we call *Shinjuku* is still part of this world. Demon City should not open its doors to them. Having let them in, they must be destroyed. By my name—"

A blazing countenance exceeding even that of Mephisto looked squarely into the eyes of the Demon City Doctor.

"—and by the name of the Demon City Doctor. Mephisto, you shall not move this girl to the general admittance wing of the hospital. Here is where you shall lie in wait for the enemy."

"That is fine with me."

"However, move the remaining patients. There is no telling what will happen next. No priority can exceed that of their extermination."

"Understood," Mephisto said with a deep bow.

"As you know, *I* do not share all the same traits as *me*. Things shall henceforth be taken care of with all due alacrity."

This much was undeniably true: Shinjuku's No. 1 P.I. and Shinjuku's Demon Physician had never before so desired the obliteration of a foe.

One summer night, two men and two women

arrived on a river that did not exist. What roles would they play upon the stage of this city? What manner of grotesque battle would unfold within its precincts?

Exactly the kind of battle that should occur here. In Demon City Shinjuku.

Part Two: Bloodsucking Belle

Chapter One

No job in Shinjuku was drearier than that of the nightshift worker, especially if that worker was a beat cop manning one of the police boxes scattered throughout the city.

After the Devil Quake, Shinjuku law enforcement had been completely reorganized. Nevertheless, many police boxes continued to operate as they always had. Even on nights when the demons were rampaging about, the three uniformed officers manning each *koban* could be observed killing time under the glow of the flickering red lights.

The commando units that patrolled the DMZ were equipped with body armor and powerful weaponry normally reserved for Special Forces units. But the police boxes were limited to the "safe areas." That was small consolation to the officers working there at night. "Safety" was a relative term in Shinjuku.

Apparitions and monsters of all stripes took those red lights as signs of human life, and an invitation to give it their best shot. A cop couldn't breathe a sigh of relief until the watercolor rays of dawn tinged the sky and the day workers streamed past the police box.

That night, Officer "Kaneda" couldn't settle down. His partners Oosugi and Wakamatsu were on patrol and wouldn't be back for another two hours.

He secured the bulletproof doors, engaged the high-tension electric fences, and turned on the monitors that scanned the streets and sidewalks around the police box. Then he sat down at the desk. But the waves of loneliness and unease gnawed at his heart and mind like an incessant car alarm.

He checked and rechecked the magazine of his gun. He inspected the incendiary and nerve gas rounds stored in the weapons locker and the 40 mm launcher. Still, he couldn't settle down.

He slapped his cheeks, bellowed out *enka* ballads, finally realized it was all for naught, and got down to analyzing the cause of his apprehensions. By now it was around midnight.

His insides were fine. He hadn't eaten anything that disagreed with him. Rather, he'd felt a bit upset earlier that evening and skipped dinner. He was A-OK now.

Rewinding the day, he couldn't come up with anything that would account for his present mood. He'd been off-duty the night before and had a bit too much to drink, but he'd completely escaped any effects of a hangover.

After thinking it over for five minutes, he finally hit on the likely cause. The day before yesterday he'd received word from the family home in Nagano. His mother's cirrhosis had worsened, and the inevitability of her condition could no longer be avoided.

He didn't think about his mother in endearing terms. Her impending death didn't arouse in him any strong feelings. What tied him in knots was what would happen *after* that.

The wife of his older brother had been pressed unwillingly into their mother's care, so they had first dibs on the house and the land it sat on. He couldn't begrudge them that right, but if the house and property turned out to be the only inheritance, well, that was another matter.

Kaneda had claims of his own to make, and it was equally unlikely that his two older sisters and two younger brothers wouldn't chime in. In any case, a simple gab-fest was unlikely to overcome the ball and chain of family ties.

In the end, it was every man for himself. Kaneda was keenly aware of this fact. If anybody started staking claims on the inheritance at his mother's deathbed, he'd have a thing or two to say about that. Simple problem, simple solution. They weren't exactly talking rocket science.

He wished somebody would visit him. Some half-woman, half-demon from the DMZ would be fine. A mugging victim would be fine. Come knocking on the door of his forlorn police box and he'd be ready with a steaming cup of tea or coffee. They'd talk the night away.

Come on down! Kaneda wished in his heart. He was going to go freaking nuts otherwise.

His wishes went unfulfilled. Only the time passed. He figured he could last an hour. And then after that, somehow hold out for another forty minutes. If his two partners would just return by then—

One o'clock in the morning. Not a sign of human life on the pavement in front of the police box.

One-thirty. The officer could believe that the red light shining onto the street was somehow alive. Come to think of it, the border where the light met the night seemed to be wavering. The soft undulations turned into a head, and the darker parts, like upside-down crescent moons, were eyes.

"Holy—" The officer blurted out, jumping to his feet.

Sitting there doing nothing, his mind was shaking free of its moorings. He was turning into the kind of *thing* more appropriate to this town.

Just then the monitors on the wall squawked an alarm. On the No. 3 monitor, a woman in a gray dress was hurrying down the dark street on the right. The street led away from the Nakai station on the Seibu Shinjuku line.

The police box was located only fifty yards from the station.

The woman looked to be in her mid-twenties. She was wearing a fair amount of makeup. Kaneda's first thought was that she worked in the "entertainment" business. Every few steps she glanced over her shoulder. She was running away from something.

Kaneda darted to the weapons locker. He pressed his palm against the handprint reader and yanked open the doors.

He got out a 12-gauge shotgun and selected a chemical incendiary load from the stack of 10-round rotary drum magazines. A hit by one of these babies triggered a chemical reaction with the creature's body fat, quickly reaching three thousand degrees and incinerating the target from within. In the case of body armor, the mist from the exploding shell would invade any breathing apparatus and deliver the same fate.

As a general rule, normal shotgun shells were used on normal human beings. During the night, though, incendiary loads were permitted. Because no normal criminal ventured out of doors in Shinjuku at night.

Kaneda released the safety.

Holding the shotgun tightly against his waist, he

ventured outside the police box.

The oppressive heat beat against his face. The woman was no more than two yards away. Even seeing him, she didn't pick up the pace.

She must be pretty calm under fire.

"Freeze!" Kaneda shouted, looking at the woman and then past her. He was doing everything according to the book. In this city, victims weren't always the ones who needed "saving." Cops were fair game too.

The woman obeyed, shooting a look behind her. Nothing was there. Her shoulders fell. Clearly from relief.

"Can I see some I.D.?" Kaneda asked politely. But he didn't relax so much as a pinky.

"Um, here you go—"

The woman turned up the right lapel of her dress. She'd stuck her I.D. there. When she lifted her collar it tumbled to the ground like a leaf. Not taking his eyes off her, Kaneda picked it up and quickly examined it.

Name: Asako Makikawa
Age: 25
Occupation: Shinjuku Traffic Center, 2nd District
Address: Shinjuku Ward, Nakaochiai 4-8-303

It looked like the real thing. The special holographic seal that only cops could distinguish was intact. Nothing was out of order.

"Okay. What's the story here?" he asked, not lowering the shotgun.

"I was at this place over by the Nakai station and it was closing time and I was on my way back, and somebody started following me. I asked who it was, but nobody answered. I started getting creeped out—"

The woman collected herself. Her breathless state and her pale face attested to her truthfulness. Kaneda raised the muzzle of the gun to the vertical.

"Well, he won't be coming after you after this. Would you like to step inside for some tea?"

The woman shook her head. "My house is pretty close. But I'd appreciate it if you could give me an escort?"

And leave my post unguarded—the thought crossed Officer Kaneda's mind.

He quickly dismissed it. "Sure. No problem."

He handed back the I.D., and set out in the lead. After about three minutes, they entered the ruined remains of a residential neighborhood. The usable concrete blocks and building materials had been carted away. All that was left—reaching out beyond the street lights—were the gaping, jagged remains of the foundations.

Curiously enough, perhaps because they reached the same height, taken all together, they looked perfectly level.

The two of them stopped in the middle of an intersection. "A lot of strange creatures nest down here," said Kaneda. "Take a left here and you can detour around them."

Asako Makikawa nodded. "But straight as the bird flies saves twenty minutes. Don't worry. They're a slow-footed, clumsy lot. If we hurry, we'll be through before they even notice."

Kaneda didn't disagree, and forged ahead at a brisk pace. For some strange reason, the street lights were all working. Still, darkness pressed in from every side, pregnant with echoes and noises. A throaty growl—fangs or claws gnashing together—pawing at the earth—

"You're not frightened?" Asako Makikawa asked behind him.

He was really getting used to the sound of her voice.

"Well, to tell the truth, it is a bit unsettling. At the end of the day, a cop is just another working stiff. What scares everybody else scares us too. I've been working at that *koban* for three and a half years now, and I'm still not used to it."

"Now that you mention it, I've had my eye on you since before I moved here." Together with the sound of her voice, he heard her opening her handbag. "I thought, 'The cop that hangs out at that police box is so young and handsome.' Nice apartment too. Your landlady told me your name, *Kaneda*-san."

"Um, that's just a nickname," the officer said sheepishly. "The guys call me 'Mr. Gold Field' because I don't like spending my money. My name's actually Hyuuga."

"Oh, is that so?" Asako said, blotting her forehead with her handkerchief. She added jokingly, "Not even on girls? That'd be a shame."

"I didn't say that." The officer lowered his voice. "I'm just happy to be able to talk to a woman like you. I've been in the mood tonight, you know? I never dreamed we'd be together this way in a place like this—"

He stopped and turned around. There wasn't a drop of sweat on his pallid face. Instead, from his unusually red lips appeared the fresh, white lines. Jagged, like the fangs of a beast.

"Y-You're a—!" Words failed her.

Asako stood rooted to the spot.

The officer spread his hands wide. The shotgun in

his right hand fell to his feet with a clatter. "Hey, hey. Let's pair up, just the two of us. We'll do it every night, here among the ruins."

The fire in Kaneda's eyes reflected in Asako's own. The moment she stared into the flames, her own will turned to cinders. She took a wavering step forward.

A glistening rivulet of drool trickled down from the corner of the cop's mouth. When that trustworthy sign of legal authority—his uniform—revealed that it housed a demon, the trap had been sprung and it was already too late. The arms of his stout frame closed around her like a pair of manacles—

The cop's body spasmed—

Abandoning his long-sought prey, the uniformed figure staggered backwards three steps, pivoting to the right.

The silhouette of his body had grown another appendage. Long and thin and sticking through his

neck. A steel rod an inch in diameter, a yard in length and drawing a straight line from end to end.

The cop turned to where the attack had come from. Where the glow from the street lights faded into the darkness stood the shadow of a man like a blue ghost.

"U-uu—v-vaasstaa—" The cop gurgled and gasped. The iron rod had torn through his larynx and mostly closed off his windpipe. *You bastard,* he intended to say.

Or perhaps it was an attempt at garbled laughter. Either way, his eyes shone like red coals as the guttural sound burbled from between his blood-coated teeth and trembling lips. More than its horrid appearance was the expression of undiluted malice and hatred. He reached out his arms like a zombie.

"C'mere. C'mere. C'mere."

Whether or not he had looked into those feral, bloodstained cat eyes—into the corrupt nature of the vampire that stole away human will—the deep blue shadow that seemed to have arisen from the ocean depths wavered like a strand of seaweed.

Abruptly the shadow spoke. "I chanced upon this young woman enjoying a midnight stroll and ended up at a police box. There I ran into this strange creature wearing a police officer's uniform. Where are you from? And what is your sire's name?"

The voice was calm, cool and collected, unlike the shadow from which it spoke.

The cop stiffened. The voice struck a chord of fear in him. But only for an instant. This child of the devil bent over and picked up the shotgun, leveled it at the shadow standing in the twilight and pulled the trigger.

Despite being a vampire—or rather *because* he was a vampire—his aim was true despite the heavy recoil.

The blue shadow wavered mightily. A second passed. And then it was engulfed in an incandescent glow. The three-thousand degree fire roasted the bones and reduced every cell to ash. For anything that was ever alive, existence became non-existence.

In a flash, the white-hot blaze wavered, and then exploded into a thousand shards of light and disappeared. Like an exquisite fireworks display. Nothing was left behind. The iron rod still stuck through his throat, the cop scanned the perimeter.

From behind, a hand slammed a white cloth against his nose and mouth. The cop clawed at the hand holding the cloth, but to no avail. It only took a second. The bloodstained eyes rolled back in their sockets. The muscles went limp. The cop collapsed to the ground in a dead faint.

A pungent odor wafted into the hot, humid night air.

"I'm not too keen on the smell either," the shadow admitted in a youthful voice. "But it's the only way to capture chaps like you alive."

The white cloth was returned to the pocket of his blue serge business suit. From its depths arose the strong smell of garlic.

Chapter Two

Setsura and Mephisto watched her closely, but nothing about Hisako Tokoyoda changed. It was two o'clock in the morning in the special containment ward on the fourth basement level of Mephisto Hospital.

The hospital was a 24/7 operation, as busy in the middle of the night as during the day. The lobby and waiting room were crowded with nightshift specialists dealing with emergency cases. The special containment ward, though, bathed in a soft blue light, was dead quiet.

On the bed, Hisako didn't move a muscle.

She hadn't budged an inch since she'd shuffled out of the way of the shaft of hot sunlight. Or to be more precise, when Setsura had visited Mephisto's office shortly before sunset, he'd informed him that she hadn't moved from the spot.

Setsura stared up at the ceiling. "This is really serious."

"Many victims bitten by vampires act like that right before the moment of death. The symptoms often get confused with ordinary illnesses."

Mephisto turned his attention to a black lacquer box sitting on his desk, a gaze that would leave even a box entranced. He asked, "How is it going? Has Shinjuku's No. 1 manhunter turned up any evidence of a handsome man wearing a black cloak?"

"Unfortunately, no clues my first day out. No other witnesses who saw the ship or those four. I inspected Fifth Street. As expected, not a drop of water is left."

"Shinjuku has swallowed them up," said Mephisto. "They are no doubt a perfect fit."

His slender white finger snaked across the lid of the box. A human finger? It had nails and joints and wrinkles. But the nails were clear as water. This was a finger so beautiful it must have been made by the gods themselves. If these fingers wounded another person, the blood would flow from the unclotting lacerations and that person would die. And while dying that person would believe himself divinely cursed.

Did the good doctor's hands even have fingerprints? Put this question to the test—look for evidence of that skin-deep physical testament to a person's unique existence—and the mark left behind would yield nothing more than a shape of the world's loveliest fingertip.

"Being able to escape the prying eyes of Setsura Aki makes them first among equals in this city."

"So how's it going on your end?" Setsura asked in a carefree voice, as if indifferent to whatever storms might be brewing in Mephisto's mind. There were echoes of a young man sauntering across an autumn field in that voice. Except that once it changed, only Mephisto truly comprehended how much it could change.

"Police and informants throughout Shinjuku have been notified to be on the lookout for a suspicious gang of four, haven't they? Let's wait for good news to filter in."

"The one thing the two of us can deservedly boast of, is how much we are of one mind when it comes to such matters."

"In other words, bupkis." Setsura sniffed. "We'll

have to hope something turns up tonight."

"That's why we're here."

"Still—" Setsura cocked his head to the side. Still, he wasn't entirely ready to go along for the ride. This was the same look he got when a batch of *senbei* didn't come out right. The fate of Shinjuku might be riding on this, and the young man valued Demon City as much as he did his *senbei*.

"You and I have investigated this thing the best we know how and came up with nothing. The prospects don't look good. What about the Toyama folks?"

"None of them has a clue. Though I haven't met with the Elder."

"You haven't?"

"He's been hibernating the last six months. Nobody knows when he's going to wake up."

"He must be dreaming one hell of a dream, you think?"

"Depends on the dream."

"I hear he turns one thousand this year. You at least have to hope that old age brings sweet dreams."

Mephisto said invitingly, "If we can't tie up the loose ends tonight, what do you say we pay him a visit?"

Setsura gave the Demon Physician a curious look. Did he really believe that an opponent bothering to pay the two of them a visit here would just walk away, scot-free?

"You getting scared?"

"Now and then. You getting brave?"

"You're the one who said we're of one mind when it comes to these things."

"It's always like this right before I zero in on the cause of the disease."

Mephisto picked up the box sitting on the table

and lifted the lid for Setsura to see. The purpose of the items wrapped in lustrous purple velvet were obvious. Two pairs of contact lenses and—

"What's this?" Setsura picked up a black tube that measured approximately a third by two-thirds of an inch.

"New earplugs my researchers came up with this morning. We both heard the sound of a koto. That got me a bit concerned. The contact lenses are there for the usual reasons."

To block the vampire "cat eye" effect.

"They seem to be able to arouse abnormalities in the visual and auditory senses. This equipment is in case our visitors show up."

"Yeah, and who's going to pay for the rehab?" Setsura intoned in a deadpan voice. "Pick a fight with senses impaired like that, and a heavyweight champ could be taken out by a blind masseuse."

"You think I've invited that kind of champion into my office?"

"I'm blushing." Setsura casually inserted the contact lenses.

Though the conversation was filled with ominous overtones, the mood in the examination room was calm and relaxed. That air of calmness filled any room these two occupied—who together symbolized all the beauty and horror that Demon City contained.

Without breaking the ambience, Setsura said, "Whip a couple of scalpels at me from back there." As if asking him to toss him a pen.

Just a couple.

"Got it." Mephisto answered with equal calm.

Shifting like a silhouette, he moved to the back of the examination room, alongside the bed. "How do they feel?" he asked, referring to the contact lenses and earplugs.

Setsura had the earplugs inserted, so the question might have struck the casual observer as a silly question for the doctor to ask.

"Everything looks blue." He added cheekily, "What was that again? I can't hear you."

"That crimson in the eyes is the source of the vampire's hypnotic abilities. The blue filter blocks it. As for the earplugs, it's up to you. You'll have to determine their effectiveness for yourself."

"And if your gizmos screw up my ears? Then what, you quack?"

"Then my fascinating collection of medical records will gain another entry," Mephisto coolly shot back.

Mephisto tossed his cape over his right shoulder. He coiled his right hand into a fist. A needle-like metal strand poked out from the center of his fist like the tip of a thin icepick. While adjusting the length of the needle for his intended purposes, he left a series of small marks on the surface of the metal with his thumbnail.

Simple scratches, but the depths of the grooves slightly differed. Setsura could see none of this. Just the Demon Physician doing what the Demon Physician always did.

"Well, then—"

"Don't wait for me. Any time."

Setsura sat back in the chair, and crossed his legs. Resting his chin against his hand and closing his eyes, he looked like a young poet waiting for the light to descend from heaven and the muse to strike.

Taking aim at the suffering young poet, Mephisto's right arm traced an arc. At the apex of the arc, a thin, silver-white line shot across the room.

Setsura extended the forefinger of the hand cupping his chin. An invisible, sub-micron titanium strand of "devil wire" shot out a yard or so in front of him, intersecting Mephisto's needle, entwining and severing it in a flash.

In the same split-second, the needle broke in two. The portion entangled in the devil wire fell away. The lower half continued on its trajectory toward Setsura. But the *senbei* shop owner somehow detected this and reacted. The tip of the devil wire turned back on itself like the head of a cobra and lunged in pursuit.

The unseen edge of the pursuing devil wire touched the remaining half of the marauding needle. The half-needle then seemed to disappear. Actually it spun to the left as the filament surged past it, bending in two and sailing on like a tiny boomerang.

What once again sent it flying past Setsura's devil wire were the small grooves left by Mephisto.

The invisible workings of Setsura's filament—the microscopic pressures and molecular ripples arising along the line, the angle of flight taken by the boomeranging needle—Mephisto predicted them ahead of time and with his elegant fingernail had encoded the instructions into the metal.

But the devil wire was hot in pursuit, and the boomerang could not compete with the air resistance. They made contact a third time. Instantly the boomerang began to spin end over end like a tiny buzzsaw, tearing into Setsura's filaments that normally would cut through any physical object.

This was the handiwork of the notches Mephisto had made. And they weren't done yet. The tips of the spinning needle flattened into scalpels that in another second would bite into Setsura's neck. And sever the carotid artery. A second had passed since they'd left Mephisto's hand.

Setsura's left hand stirred. It was over. The needle stopped in mid-air. Pinned between his thumb and forefinger.

Viewed by any bystander, it would be a rather anticlimactic conclusion. Only the two of them knew that when they played, they always played for keeps.

"You were a little slow there," Mephisto said lightly. "Must be because of the heat." Truth was, he'd intended the needle more as simple target practice.

"You ain't kidding. That was a sorry performance, if I say so myself." Setsura shrugged. "It's always darkest before it goes completely black. We'll pin our hopes on Doctor Mephisto's supernatural skills."

"The sun sets at six-thirty," Mephisto said, not looking at the clock. "Still, a wire wrangler off his game is better than none. We should decamp to the basement."

Setsura smirked. "Well said."

There was just one thing different now about the empty examination room the two of them were standing in. A crescent-shaped strand of needle-like metal was sitting on the desk. The light of the setting sun pouring through the windows stained it red.

Several seconds after Setsura and Mephisto left, a fresh cut appeared in the needle, and it split down the middle into two pieces.

The special containment ward. Two o'clock in the morning.

Mephisto leaned against the wall and glanced at the door. Sitting on the sofa, Setsura was as still as a statue. Only his eyes were peeled.

"They're coming," he said.

There wasn't an outside monitor in the hospital room. The alloy-steel, nuclear blast-hardened walls were airtight as well. And yet somehow he knew.

"In the vicinity of the elevator. Getting closer. A man, and not a bad-looking man at that."

"He took the elevator? What are the security details doing?"

"Probably wondering what all that big budget high tech is good for."

Setsura turned to the side, as did Mephisto, looking at Hisako Tokoyoda who was beginning to stand up on the bed. Not gracefully. She braced her legs and drew herself to her full height. Her eyes alone were downcast. Her hair dangled in stringy strands from her head.

Even from where Setsura and Mephisto were standing, they couldn't read the expression on her face.

Her shoulders shook. It was only a long moment later that they realized she was laughing silently. She extended her arm from the sleeve of her hospital gown. Dark blue veins ran down the singer's cadaverous arms.

The slumped head spoke. "They're beyond the door. They're calling to me. They're calling to me. I must go."

Hisako got down from the bed. A heavy noise resounded. Neither of her observers moved.

Hisako approached the door. She reached out toward the white surface and pushed. It didn't budge. She shoved. Nothing moved. She continued to press against it. Something out there was beckoning her. Locked inside this small fortress, she somehow comprehended that.

Kiiii—kiiii—kiiii—

A sound like fingernails on a blackboard as Hisako clawed at the steel alloy door. And didn't leave a trace. No—she left behind a thin trail of vermillion. She'd torn away a nail.

She continued to scratch at the door with a perverse persistence. The mark of the vampire's victim. Even knowing the dark fate that awaited them, they could not put off the doomed reunion. And if the visitor could not come, then the victim would surely go.

"Open the door." Setsura gestured with his eyes. "As things stand now, the guy out there isn't getting in either."

"You mean, the fellow who made it *this* far." Mephisto calmly replied, his cool gaze not straying away from Hisako.

"If you don't let her out, you won't have anything new for your case files."

No matter how tragic the circumstances, this doctor valued nothing as much as his case files. At the end of the day, proving his diagnosis and providing a cure pretty much exhausted the Demon Physician's ethical reservoirs.

"You know—"

Setsura had turned to Mephisto when Hisako stopped struggling against the door. The door and her gown were dark with blood. Her hands fell limply to her sides. She stared at the door. Then she slowly turned to them.

Neither Mephisto nor Setsura could read the look on her face. It was difficult to imagine any human being wearing such an expression. Burning red eyes below raised eyebrows. Two fangs protruding from turned-up lips. She was already no longer human. This alone was enough to create a lifetime of nightmares.

But the real horror was in the way she gazed at them, eyes roiling with poisonous hate. *"Let me out. Let me out of here. So he can drink my blood."*

Hisako raised her arms in front of her. Her fingers bent like hooks, covered with blood. Her red eyes shifted from their faces to her own fingertips.

Her countenance dissolved into indescribable lust. She raised her hands to her mouth. Her maroon tongue parted her lips and licked at her fingers. Vulgar greed was an entirely human trait. The monstrous avarice on Hisako's face was many times worse than that. If this woman's mother were present, she would demand her daughter's death and search for a weapon herself.

Her lips now dyed darker than her fingers, Hisako closed her eyes in bliss.

She opened her eyes and stared at the two men. "Did you enjoy that?" Doctor Mephisto asked, in the manner of a professor querying a student. Whether he'd ever been one was anybody's guess.

"Delicious," she answered at once.

"Do you imagine your own blood can satisfy you?" Mephisto continued in the same indifferent voice. His was a cold and clinical examination, as if made by some stainless steel mechanism smelted from cursed ore at midnight.

"Well—" Her voice trailed off. She smiled sweetly. A cherubic smile that her eyes alone didn't share. "The blood of others should taste *so* much better."

"Do you hear that?" Mephisto turned to Setsura. "The first bit of new information this incident has produced. Not yet a vampire—very close to becoming one—and yet she has an opinion about the taste of her own blood. I've never seen that before."

"If you say so," Setsura said sourly. He shot back a

look that said, *Quit yanking my chain.* With the earplugs in, he couldn't hear a thing Mephisto's patient said.

Hisako came closer. She walked with a strangely relaxed gait, as if meeting a long-lost lover she hadn't seen in a lifetime. Befitting her appearance all the more, she held her hands out in front of her like a singer. "Your blood would be even better. Such pretty, beautiful people—"

"Well, then—" Mephisto started to say.

It was enough to make Hisako freeze. The devilish hunger was overtaken by pure terror.

"You are still my patient. The cause of your illness is outside. How about a brief get-together before we cure you?"

Speaking in almost disinterested tones, without a touch of arrogance, and not sparing Hisako a second glance, Mephisto turned toward the door. A faint melody drifted through the walls. A tune played on a koto. Both Mephisto and Setsura reeled from the shock. The sweet reverberations somehow leaked into this airtight vault.

That by itself wouldn't have been so amazing—were it not for the earplugs. The koto's melody thrummed directly against their eardrums and at the same time clouded their thoughts.

Nobody in Shinjuku would have believed it, but Setsura Aki and Doctor Mephisto were forced to their knees.

"This is—" Mephisto half-closed his eyes. It was a miracle his voice was not similarly muddied. "If I fall asleep before you, try to give me an accurate report of how much longer you last—"

Even collapsed on the floor, the body clothed in white looked elegant and beautiful.

"Dumb quack." On his knees, supporting himself

with his left hand, Setsura looked toward the door and cursed him.

"I've taken steps in case of an emergency—but just in case—I'll waive the hospital bills—" Mephisto's eyelids closed.

The door slid to the right. Hisako smiled broadly. A silhouette standing in the hallway was the last thing impressed onto his consciousness as Setsura slumped to the floor.

The delicate notes of the koto echoed eerily inside the small room. What was this weapon that so easily felled Demon City's two princes of darkness, the two that nobody else dared lay a finger on? And what being wielded it?

The shadow in the corridor didn't move. A throaty voice issued forth in Chinese. "Formidable opponents. With them here, I could not open the door by myself. Men who truly belong to this city. However—" He stopped speaking and turned to Hisako. "The ghost koto *Silent Night* conquers all. When it is heard, men must sleep. Come."

That word was her command. Like a marionette dangling from his strings, Hisako stepped waveringly into the hallway. She stood beside the silhouette, reached up with her stained hands and tore apart her gown, exposing her emaciated breasts. Her ribs showed through her pale skin.

"Pitiful." There was sorrow in his voice. "But your beauty shall soon be restored. The beauty of our world is greater than you can imagine."

Under the cold fluorescent lights, the black shadow enveloped the white figure.

Seconds passed.

The fused silhouettes splintered into a kaleidoscope

of colors. The man's voice said, "The men in the hospital room—make them your lovers."

"Yes," Hisako answered in Japanese. She spoke with a reanimated vigor. Her countenance possessed a captivating beauty.

Except that it would be different if this strength truly arose from within. Something was *off* about the bright, carefree voice. Some deeply-rooted part of her had turned bad and ugly. The only thing enlivening her now was the cold, dark night.

The cheek facing the hospital room door was as rounded as a peach. The flesh and muscles of her throat were firm and supple, her exposed breasts ripe and full. Hisako passed through the doorway.

No scars marred her lovely neck. According to folklore, the teeth marks borne by the victim vanished at *that* moment—the moment at which the prey became the predator.

She looked down at Setsura and Mephisto, this lovely flower of the nightclubs now brimming with shadows. She smiled a smile a hundred times more grotesque than when she'd been wasting away. Her fangs were longer and sharper too.

The dreadful countenance of the former singer shone as she licked her lips in anticipation. Her supple limbs trembled in anticipation of the waiting feast.

She took another step forward.

Chapter Three

Mephisto Hospital never closed. Mechanical versions of the five senses watched over the facilities every minute of the day.

The access routes boasted geometrically-aligned sensor arrays customized to cover a large hospital. Labyrinthine hallways penetrated the facilities. The examination rooms were furnished with state-of-the-art equipment. And then there were the mysterious places nobody but the hospital director knew the reason for—

Everywhere, countless eyes and ears extended the range of every defensive perimeter.

The electronic sensors that made up these "five senses" could detect subtle shifts in light like the eyes of an artist. Could sense with the ears of a master musician the sound a pin makes falling on plush carpet. Could sniff out chemical changes in the air equal to the nose of a perfumer—

And so on and so forth.

When that young man walked through the front lobby and the first-floor waiting room, the sensors did not record a single abnormality. Because it didn't detect any.

Not because he was the same as any other person. And not because he wasn't. It was meaningless to talk about "distinctions." When he walked in, the receptionist noted his presence. The patients sitting in the vestibule saw him coming as well. Nothing about him looked "off."

In this city, in this hospital, he was utterly "normal."

But the electric eyes and ears and noses did not detect him. Not because there was nothing "wrong." But because there was nothing "right" to compare him to.

The cameras didn't "see" him. The thermal scanners didn't "feel" his body heat. The microphones didn't "hear" footsteps, a beating heart, blood pumping through arteries and veins. His was an existence without color or smell or shape or sound. He wasn't there. And the result was that the security center wasn't notified and the mechanical defense perimeters weren't activated.

Only the human beings noticed him. With hardly a glance at the receptionist, knowing where he was going, he headed to the elevators with a calmly self-assured stride.

"Wait just a minute," the receptionist called out cheerfully.

He didn't stop. As soon as he moved from the lobby into the hospital proper, he stepped into a web of sensors. But other than not stopping for the receptionist, there wasn't a thing wrong with the visitor. He wasn't carrying weapons or even a cell phone.

So the young lady hesitated making the call that would enforce her request. Then with her tongue, she flicked a small switch in one of her molars and instructed the security guards to detain the man. There were ten people waiting in the lobby. Two quickly got up and approached him.

"We're sorry, but you need to check in at the front desk."

The words had barely left his mouth when he collapsed to the floor. The remaining guard was about to spring into action. The receptionist reached for the panic button. In that instant, a sweet melody drifted through the lobby.

Doctor Mephisto was the first one to regain consciousness. He'd been the first one to lose consciousness, and all things in their order. He took note of Setsura lying next to him, but didn't get up. He lay there and cast his eyes around the room.

Five seconds later, Setsura opened his eyes. Exactly the same amount of time that had passed after Mephisto had fainted. There did seem to be some sort of *simpático* vibe between them.

But their reactions were quite different. Like a straight-A student who'd made a careless mistake, Mephisto carefully examined his neck and announced, "You're fine. Neither you nor I appear to have been bitten. I'll do a more thorough examination later, but a security check first."

"So it seems," said Setsura, quickly patting himself down. His eyes narrowed. "Nine minutes past two. A bit over eight minutes since you collapsed. That music knocks you out quick, but the effects don't last long once you can't hear it anymore."

"There's something I'm not getting."

"Eight minutes, four seconds. Seven minutes fifty-nine seconds for me."

"You lasted five seconds longer," Mephisto murmured. "What did you do?"

His eyes fell on the floor before him. The location where the vampire Hisako had advanced towards them. A horrifying scene.

Supposing it had a head, the gowned torso lay "face down" on the floor, in a sea of blood a good yard in diameter and at least a quarter-inch deep. All four quarts of blood that had once been inside Hisako were now outside her.

The head sat at Setsura's feet, quietly staring into space. "Exactly according to tradition," he quipped.

The relaxed, melancholic look etched on her face was the same as it had been the night before, and at the nightclub in Kabuki-cho.

"Release those filaments of yours. They're dangerous. When did you string them up?"

"When I figured she'd be coming back," Setsura said indifferently. He waved his left hand. The devil wires that had saved their lives—spared them the fate of becoming part of her vampire brood—vanished invisibly into his fist.

A single step was all it had taken to sever Hisako's head from her body.

"Now we know that their eyesight isn't any better than ours."

"Good to know. But we should stake the body afterwards just to make sure."

From time immemorial, vampires had been dispatched with a stake through the heart. Then decapitation after that. They'd be doing it in reverse order, but the end was what mattered, not the means.

Mephisto shook his head as he peered down at the floor. "For now it seems that my fate is having to listen to you preen instead. Here's another piece of evidence."

"Fingers." Setsura squatted down to get a better look.

The long, gray digits lay scattered several inches away from the pool of gore. Three fingers. Two had already decayed past recognition. The remaining finger retained its delicate, sculpture-like form. The gray nail and the creases in the knuckles were still distinct. Focus the eyes hard enough and even the tiny spikes of hair were visible.

Quite definitely fingers.

"When a vampire loses a part of his body, it reverts to its natural age. This according to tradition also."

Mephisto nodded stiffly. Though listening attentively, he seemed to be there in body but not in spirit.

"The guy in the hallway must have intended her to take our blood. Except that she lost her head instead. And when he instinctively reached out to see what was going on, he added his fingers to the body count."

Setsura related the alarming facts with an almost bored air. There was no way to align his reaction with the facts before their faces. If tonight's visitor was a demon, then the same applied to this beautiful manhunter.

"If we suppose that he took off after losing the fingers, we could probably conclude that her sire would have a hard time reviving himself if he lost his head as well. He may even feel pain. Any data from Toyama about vampires parting with a hand or foot?"

Mephisto didn't answer, and Setsura turned to look at him. A tense shadow passed across the empty look on Mephisto's face. He stared at the closed door. What froze Setsura where he stood was the taut sense of disquiet rising from his white-clothed frame.

A *something* was swirling about the briny, blood-drenched room.

"Hey, take it easy."

It came straight at him and Setsura held up his hands to ward it off. His skin prickled and his hair stood on end. He instinctively concentrated on keeping the ink-black thing boiling up from his guts in check.

It was fear. Anger. Doctor Mephisto's anger tasted like fear to Setsura Aki.

Mephisto said, in a voice that sounded like the dead come back to life, "I waited. I waited in order to ascertain the source of the patient's illness. It came as far as that door. And then left with the patient dead and it losing a couple of fingers. It left because of your power. What did I do? Nothing. I fainted on the floor. Any possibility of treatment slipped through these hands. I was saved by your filaments, which killed the patient."

He turned to Setsura, and there was that look in his eyes.

"Enough already," said Setsura, waving his hands. Whatever *simpático* feeling the two of them had shared, the hospital director was turning into another creature entirely.

Mephisto said, "I do not want you leaving here. No one can know that Doctor Mephisto was so completely powerless in the face of a patient's death. That means that I can't let you out of this hospital—out of this room."

"So no good deed goes unpunished. That puts a person such as *I* in something of a bind." Setsura spoke softly. "I would ask you not to level such strange accusations at *me*."

An entirely different atmosphere now enveloped the room. It emanated from Setsura. As with Mephisto, this vibe that was Setsura but *not* Setsura was suffused with an extraordinary sense of being that could not be taken lightly.

No resident of Demon City honestly wished to witness it with their bare eyes. But what they all secretly pined for down in the darkest depths of the soul had sprung into reality.

It'd been a long time since Mephisto had smiled so broadly. "But right now, I need you like I have never needed you before," he said in dark tones. "In order to eliminate the source of the infection, it must first be located. I believe that this incident will rock the foundations of Shinjuku. Sooner or later, the mayor would have hired you to track it down. But no need for that now. My commission will suffice. Find them. Those remaining three. And leave the rest to me."

The intention of Mephisto's commission was more to salve his wounded pride and restore his disgraced honor to its shining former self than it was to serve the peace and security of Shinjuku. Anybody being told by him to "leave the rest to me" could sleep well at night.

There was no way to interpret Setsura's reaction. The expression on his face was as impassive as Doctor Mephisto's ever was. Setsura said, the look in his eyes not gaining a single degree of warmth, "I will think it over. I dislike associating with excitable clients. Right now that includes you. Call me once you have calmed down. Then I shall do as I see fit."

"I couldn't ask for anything more," agreed Mephisto. "Well, I need to figure out why, from the time it entered until the time it left, our defenses did nothing. And you?"

"I am going home to get some sleep. Tomorrow is another working day." Setsura's gaze lingered for a sad moment on Hisako's body lying on the floor as he turned toward the door. He glanced back over his shoulder. "Once you understand how it got in, give me a ring, okay?"

His curt way of saying, *Sorry, but I'm not sticking around to keep you company.*

Shooting the departing figure a look, Mephisto said

to himself, "That's why I don't care for the *normal* him." He wasn't kidding. "Well, then." With Setsura gone, he returned his attention to the decaying remains at his feet. An analysis might reveal the owner's age or cellular structure. This was the kind of thing he only trusted himself to get right.

"A vampire, eh? And one of Eastern extraction at that. Perhaps living out a long-held dream."

His eyes gleamed with an unnatural light. Many a page in the hidden histories of the world were devoted to those with eyes like his. Those who, enchanted by the mysteries blossoming in those forbidden zones, bartered away body and soul and stepped into the unknown.

Such as Paracelsus or Doctor Faust or Josef Mengele.

But none of their eyes shone as brightly as his. Mephisto's eyes didn't only brim with the light of knowledge tearing apart the curtains of ignorance. But also with a darkness as deep as hell itself.

The breeze whipped at his duster as Setsura exited the hospital lobby. Leaving the hospital grounds, he stopped. For some reason, the comely young man stood rooted to the spot. It was almost as if, among all the people walking past him on the sidewalk, an even more remarkable countenance than his own had made its presence known.

The city was alive before his eyes. Taxi cabs picked up men and women of questionable character and sped off. Flickering "Vacancy" signs illuminated the entrances of the capsule hotels. Kids up to no good flocked around the all-night fast food joints and convenience stores.

Out in front of the bars and peep shows and strip

clubs, the barkers and bouncers bartered with the passersby, offering for sale every imaginable flavor of the weird and the perverse.

An ugly shadow flitted across his feet. Above his head floated a big, carpet-like creature. It dove down, grabbed a rat-sized animal and soared back into the air.

A bunch of gangbangers straddling supercharged minibikes just as suddenly found their vision totally obstructed. With yells and the squealing of brakes, bikes rolled. The tanks ruptured and burst into flames.

With uncannily good timing, another figure darted in, this one a freelance doctor or lawyer, who'd probably released the flying carpet bait from his bulging pockets.

A star pattern of laser light burst from the windows of a building facing Yasukuni Avenue. A scream followed. Strands of the brilliant blue light flashed through the buildings and disappeared. Perhaps a burglar trying to knock off a loan shark operation had encountered a carnivorous creature trained as a watchdog.

The city was alive. No matter how hideous, Shinjuku would do its level best to make the wishes of its residents come true. But now a cold wind was blowing, and only Setsura could read its tints and hues.

Two women whose dress made their disreputable occupation obvious eyed Setsura, and then passed by without the slightest sign of interest.

The exquisite manhunter stood there, a statue of ice. That's what a wind like this would do. In time, it would circle Shinjuku and paint all of God's creatures, great and small, the same color. The color of blood and darkness.

That was the premonition he felt. He couldn't say

how much time they had left. Brushing the sweltering hot air aside, Setsura walked toward Yasukuni Avenue.

He had to get down to business and didn't have a moment to lose. He was starting to believe that even in midsummer, the nights in this city somehow lasted longer than the days.

Part Three: Red Fang

Chapter One

The darkness was nowhere and everywhere. If he extended his grasp, reached down deeper and deeper, it grew so thick he imagined closing his fist and tearing pieces of it away.

The darkness came in many varieties. Those who lived in it developed by necessity the ability to discern among them. Its voices, scents, thoughts. And more than anything else, its passions.

This was the same darkness that had surrounded the Tower of London and cloaked the condemned trudging to the gallows steeped in grudges and profound regrets. Their jailers wisely kept their distance. They'd learned by experience what it meant to be so possessed.

The darkness watched over the dance of life—the summer festivals, the campfires, the choruses of friends and lovers—and breathed life into the souls of its new visitors.

The passions, joys, angers, sorrows and fears of humans, plants and animals alike—the darkness absorbed them, digested them, seasoned them over time, and thus determined the essence of its own nature.

For eons the darkness had continually consumed blood and wickedness and all their unquenchable thirsts, growing as constricted in its senses and emotions as it was vast and unlimited.

Somewhere in the darkness a voice asked, "Is that you, Ryuuki?"

The dusty, archaic Chinese would demand a skilled linguist to calculate which ancient era it came from.

"Yes." The shadow that had visited Mephisto Hospital.

The owners of both voices sank down in the eternal black.

"You failed?"

"I failed." In that same tone of voice.

"How about that." This hoarse voice echoed surprise. "You and *Silent Night* encountered a substantial obstacle?"

"Including the loss of my fingers."

"And what trick accomplished that?"

"I do not know. The woman I summoned lost her head. I instinctively reached out and the same thing happened to my fingers. Thinking about it now, I believe that something like a *mist blade* was strung through the air."

"This sounds like the kind of wizardry wielded by Yang Dan during the Wei Dynasty. Though, in that case, it should have been visible to your eyes."

"Kikiou-sama, it was—" The hesitation in the young voice stirred the darkness.

"What?"

"I believe the wielder of that weapon was the same man in black we saw when we arrived."

"Well—"

A long silence followed, that would have left any person in a profound state of unease. "Him? I could believe it if it was him. After two thousand years, visiting this city most suited to our needs, we make the first person we encounter into an enemy and a most formidable enemy at that. Is this also part of the cycle of rebirth?"

The younger voice remained silent this time. He was either unable to ascertain the intent of the older man's questions, or understanding them, did not know how to respond.

"But we will win," the older one continued. "Hasn't it always been so? We have come this far by knowing more about our enemies than they know about us. Our knowledge is informed by our superior intelligence. More than any place we have been before, this is a city we can wear like a second skin. We will stir and boil the blood and evil just as Emperor Jin did in his human cauldrons. It might have been a mistake to allow you to sate your hunger so soon after we arrived. But knowing the strength of this new enemy will prove useful. The sooner we dispose of those two, the better."

"Understood." A firm statement, unburdened by resentment or hatred. An affirmative answer, even.

"Oh, yes."

The older man spoke a bit overdramatically. "Even that man Shuuran took as her lover that first night was struck down."

The astonishment rippled through the darkness. "That means that in a single night, both of our thralls were—"

"That's exactly what it means. Shuuran, though, did not lose any digits in the process. That is because, not being a slave to the old ways, she made him her own right from the start."

"I understand what you are saying, but—" There was a stubborn resolve in the younger man's voice. "It is a long-established custom of our kind that we repeatedly visit our thralls."

"Visit them a hundred times and the results will be the same." Resolve filled the old man's voice. "How many times have you died and reincarnated? Do not lightly set aside the suffering and fires of hell that make us long for extinction. It would be one thing if we were still living during the Hsia or Shang Dynasties. But to those familiar with our ways, a second visit is only an opportunity to lay a trap."

The loathing in the old man's voice was as sharp and penetrating as a needle. *To die and reincarnate.* What strange words they were when taken at face value.

If this repeated visiting of the victim had the power of inviolable law, then those strictly adhering to it should rise to supremacy. In which case, no matter what creature of the night, none would succumb, even when caught unawares.

Assuming the old man was right, that meant that the young man had died and been reborn any number of times; that meant there were no special measures a vampire could take to avoid death if the proper blow was delivered. And it meant that once reincarnated, the mortal body did not put on immortality.

"That may be correct," the young man said. "However—"

He was about to launch into a heated dispute when a third voice disturbed the gloom.

"A fine piece of work there, Ryuuki."

The speaker was a woman. The enchanting reverberations of her youthful, vibrant voice electrified the night and made their eyes stare uselessly into the black.

"It has been a long time. I want a good look at you. Come along."

"Princess—" The equivocations in the hoarse voice

were apparent. "I was going to report to you later. Ryuuki has committed a grave error."

"I know. I've been listening. And I'm certain that you knew as well."

There was laughter in her voice. The elegance of its entrancing echoes seemed to spring from her innate disposition.

"Please forgive me."

"Ha. How about that, Kikiou? An old man like you despising the rites of the brood while a youngster like Ryuuki adheres to them. Well, it's all the same to me. Don't keep me waiting, Ryuuki. I'll hold Kikiou responsible if you're late."

"I understand," the ancient voice said hastily. His tension raised his pitch a notch.

From somewhere there came the sense of people standing. At length, the sound of a hinge turning. Blue light contended with the ink-dark world.

The being that belonged to the voice called Ryuuki entered the room and quietly shut the door. Turning around, he sank to one knee and bowed deeply. The door was made of thick wood, driven through with iron-black nails. Marble tiles covered the floor.

He was in a blue world. The blue of the deepest ocean depths streamed through the windows, the blue before the rushing, pounding waves swept everything away.

It was a large and magnificent room, at least twenty feet wide by thirty feet long, accented with rugs and decorative tables and chairs. Lining the wall were a six-legged Chinese-style chest and incense burners. The priceless value of these treasures was clear from the first glance. They were so realistically carved with pictures of phoenixes, dragons, sea serpents and lions that an admirer of art could believe that touching one of their fangs would draw blood.

Standing among them, the young man's shadow stretched out across the floor.

A strange smell filled the room. It came from the bronze incense burners on the tables and standing next to the walls. The sour edge to the thick odor suggested they were not the sole source of the smell.

"Is that you, Ryuuki?" asked the woman from before, her voice touched with inebriation.

"Yes."

"Come over here."

"Yes."

The young man got to his feet. Standing in his way were two objects. A large Buddha statue glittered golden in the blue light. Beyond that was an elliptical pavilion.

The statue lay on the floor. It was six feet long. Its surface twinkled like stars. Considering its owner, that it was dressed in gold was no surprise. It was covered from head to toe in leaves of gold foil. Hundreds, if not thousands of these leaves clothed the adult-sized statue like magical golden scales.

A jade burial robe had been discovered in the mausoleum of a Han Dynasty noble in Hebei Province, Mancheng County. The elliptical gemstones were stitched together with gold and silver threads. The jewels were said to come from the enchanted lands of the Kunlun Mountains and could bestow the power of immortality.

Those who wore it sought life after life, so that being dead they would not die.

Replacing the jewels in the robe with gold made

the statue near where Ryuuki was standing all the more opulent and beautiful. It was an article of rare beauty shrouded by the scent of raw avarice.

The silk pavilion wavered in the uncertain shadows. The blue light warped its shape like a palace submerged beneath the sea. Before Ryuuki's eyes, the seamless fabric parted to the right and left. The rich fragrance weighed down the air. This was the source of that mysterious smell.

The sound of falling water rang out.

Ryuuki knelt and bowed reverentially to the beings enshrined at the back of the pavilion.

Shining eyes bright with evil, fangs like small mountain peaks projecting from a mouth like the slit of a mountain gorge, abdomen and limbs covered with lizard's scales—possessing both a remorseless ferocity and a divine bearing unlike that of any mortal animal. A creature from out of the legends. A dragon.

And not just one. Forefeet pawing the earth, heads raised and glaring contemptuously at the world, the four magical creatures faced outward in the directions of the compass, each standing over twelve feet in height.

Ryuuki didn't move.

The eyes of the giant dragons were crimson rubies, the fangs and claws white bronze. This was a sculpture. The torsos of the dragons overlapped each other, together forming a golden bathtub. The necks and heads soared up from the rim.

At that moment arose the face of the most beautiful woman in the world. The woman who had sailed on Fifth Street toward Shinjuku singing that haunting song. Every *princess* who deserved the name was her.

"It's been a long time since the two of us have spoken like this."

She smiled, baring her white teeth. So white they almost made Ryuuki wince. Teeth as savage as they were sublime. Anyone looking upon her could not help but imagine those teeth sinking into his own neck. In a trance, he would undo his collar and expose his throat for it.

Ryuuki bowed his head and did not move, the posture taken by the loyal servant before his master.

"Raise your head and look at me," she said in brooding tones.

He did as he was told.

Two blue serpents lazily coiled down the side of the bathtub. From her arms. The dark red rivulets tore apart, divided again and then again, the flow thickening as it ran along.

"I expected you to make a mistake like that."

"There's nothing I can say," Ryuuki said somberly.

"Kikiou's anger is understandable. It's *them.* We intended to draw this city into our domain before they grew wise to our presence. Whatever wisdom two thousand years have imparted to him, whom am I to disagree?"

Ryuuki again had nothing to say in reply.

"Ryuuki," she asked in a serious voice, "what do you think of this city?"

"What do I think?"

"Kikiou says it is a city most appropriate to our needs."

"Then so would I."

"I'm not so sure."

"Then neither am I."

There was not a particle of difference between the two answers.

He meant both from the bottom of his heart.

"It is very quiet." She closed her eyes. The words almost became a song. "But Kikiou finds the quiet disquieting. So do I. To be free—to act as we wish to our heart's content—to feed the hunger of body and soul—will somebody dare stand in our way?"

The red water fell from her fingers like a thread. It fell onto the head of a dragon, trickled across the uneven surface, and ran into the dragon's eyes. There the colors blended together. A slippery red mass rose up. Her limbs. The red film split apart exposing the white skin beneath as it washed off in splotches. The undeniable smell filled the blue air.

The smell of blood. Fresh blood covered her like a second skin. She was soaking in a golden bathtub filled with blood, a sight as horrific as it was befitting her.

At the end of the sixteenth century, in the northwestern part of Hungary known as the Little Carpathians, Countess Elizabeth Bathory was rumored to have preserved her beauty and youth with fresh blood. Through the beginning of the seventh century, she slaughtered upwards of fifty girls from the surrounding villages for that purpose.

According to court records from the period, the girls were stripped, tortured in ways too grotesque to describe, and then cut apart. The overflowing blood was collected in buckets by the servants, and used to fill the bath where "Countess Dracula" washed herself in order to preserve her eternal beauty. Because she believed that blood was life.

This enchanting woman from the Orient was using blood for the same purpose. After Elizabeth Bathory's evil games came to light, "Countess Dracula" was sealed inside her blood-smeared bedroom and eventually died there.

However, the means of stealing away the life of *this* woman remained undiscovered. Coming into contact with the woman known as "Princess," these vast pools of blood were invigorated by her demonic qualities and reinvigorated her in turn.

She bent over, dipped her hands into the blood and raised them up. And brought her mouth up to the blood trickling from her cupped hands, purring as she drank. A lewd and lascivious slurping sound.

The crimson coated her white throat, quivering breasts, and sleek stomach, and stained the dense black bush between her thighs.

"*Ahh*—" she moaned, rubbing her body with blood. "Look at me, Ryuuki. Don't avert your eyes. Look at me with those eyes, eyes filled forever with cold desire, and watch what I do. You whose body had already let go of life and every ounce of its heart and soul in the palace of Emperor Zheng. All the more reason it sets me on fire."

Blood frothed and foamed at her mouth. She squeezed her breasts, breasts she had grown as if only for his delight. She pressed her fingers into the skin for him to see, kneading the flesh as she stroked her nipples. The smell of blood arose from her hands and chest.

Her moist eyes gazed playfully at Ryuuki as her fingers trailed down her belly. Slipping them deep inside herself, she raised a hoarse cry.

"Listen—"

The wet, sucking noise mingled with her voice. The sound of her blood-soaked fingers caressing the folds of her blood-drenched privates.

"*Ahh*—" she groaned, soaring towards the heights of ecstasy.

The sound was calculated to capture the attention of any man. A man with a will of iron turned to putty in her hands. A single utterance reduced him to an animal driven by its basest instincts, wanting nothing in the world except to mount her.

Her free hand circled her back where her bottom awaited. She didn't hesitate, plunging in her finger, all the way in, and commenced vigorously pumping it in and out.

"It really is better with a man," she gasped, her back arching. Her fingers filled both of her clefts. "A man's is better. Emperor Jie had a fine one indeed. So did Emperor Zhou. I wouldn't even mind Emperor You's. But now, only those dark eyes of yours can see what I have to offer. How I hate that. That is why I came here. To this wicked city—" She chuckled. "Overflowing with so much debauchery."

She stepped out of the tub, continuing to grope herself. The steaming blood pattered onto the dragon's head and neck. Red splotches flowered on the floor as she made her way to where Ryuuki still crouched like an immovable rock. His eyes looked straight at her crotch, eyes filled with cold desire.

"Eat me," she ordered him. She stood with her feet planted a shoulder's width apart.

No matter how faithful a servant, no man could obey such a command except in the depths of humiliation. But her faithful retainers could do nothing but attend to her words.

"Hurry. Do it hard."

She thrust her hips forward. A translucent, viscous liquid—other than the blood—ran down her thighs. Her countenance and bearing—bristling with noble elegance—would alone stand every hair on the average man on end.

Ryuuki nodded, and pressed his face into the valley between her widely-spread legs. She seized hold of the young man's head, flung back her own and let out a small scream. The sound of lips against flesh sang out like a musical instrument.

"You loathsome, damnable man!" she cried out, tossing her hair. She laughed. Her smile could throw a shadow across the sun. "You've died for me so many times, and still I cannot call you mine. That is why I'll never let you go. I'll never let you sleep. No matter how many times you go down on me, I'll never make you fuck me. I know why you slunk back here after losing your fingers. *Ahh*—Stick it in my ass."

His right hand circled her ripe derriere. She had a most charming backside, slippery and glistening. At a touch, her skin popped with the fresh elasticity of a virgin, the oils and natural lubricants poured from her. There wasn't a man alive who couldn't eat her the whole night long and never tire of the feast.

Her ass was as tight as a drum, hardly ready to admit a darning needle let alone a finger.

Ryuuki thrust in his finger. He had a strong hand and his thumb was there to assist. The remaining digits rose no higher than his fist. They showed their smooth, delicate stumps and then vanished from view. She pursed her lips and bowed her back in the face of a strength that brooked no resistance in her tender flesh.

Her cruel mouth parted, revealing her two fangs. Her eyes glowed with red fire. The face of pure devilry. Her fangs were crimson as well. But not because they were coated in blood. They were red in their essence.

She moaned. Lowering her head, she cupped her breasts, lifted them up, and pierced them with her fangs. The blood erupted as if from a punctured hose. She lapped at the fresh blood oozing over the dried gore, as Ryuuki's arousing caresses continued.

She gave him her sex and her ass. And still unsatisfied, sank her own tusks into her own breasts. Less a woman than a living beast.

"Kill him!" she screamed. "The man who took your fingers. Kill him so that I may reign over this city! He has aroused in me a most terrible enemy!"

Chapter Two

The next day, Aki Senbei had a visitor. Setsura was rolling up the steel shutters. The electric motor had given out two weeks before. Leaving it unrepaired added another five minutes to accomplish the task.

He had his shoulder into it and the shutters a third of the way up when a cheerful voice behind him said, "Look at that. A true Tokyoite."

Setsura lost his balance. It wasn't his fault. The visitor hadn't made any noise and Setsura hadn't sensed her sneaking up. But what really threw him off his stride was the random nature of the statement.

He braced himself against the shutters and turned around. "Well, well," he said, not so much an expression of annoyance as delighted surprise at an unexpected reunion.

Standing about a yard from him, wearing a moss-green dress, was the girl who'd gotten herself nice and plastered at the bar on Fifth Street. Setsura smiled. His smile was always friendly and welcoming. The look of apprehension on the girl's face dissolved into a grin.

Her oval face and the way her hair was tied up with a ribbon suggested a woman in her twenties. The body-hugging dress accentuated the ample bust and rounded hips that lent her five-foot six-inch frame a generous physicality. The purse hanging loosely from her belt and the blue scarf tied around her neck suggested a kind of practiced innocence, the kind often seen in sophisticated college coeds.

"Um, I'm the girl who had a bit too much to drink at the bar on Fifth Street," she admitted awkwardly.

"I am a Tokyoite, but I wasn't born in Kanda City." Setsura gave up on the shutters for the time being. "Did you find your way home okay?"

Soon after he'd watched the mysterious ship sail out of sight, the girl had been bundled into a taxi and was soon snoring heartily away.

"Eh, more or less." She hesitated, and then added cheerfully, "I dumped him."

An otherwise inappropriate subject to bring up with a total stranger, but not so strange seeing that she was talking to Setsura.

"That's too bad. You gotta feel sorry for the guy."

"It's okay. He didn't take me home in that condition. We somehow ended up at a hotel. Fortunately, I'd sobered up enough by that point. I slapped him and took off."

"Oh." Setsura gave the girl a rueful look. It was hard to tell whether she or her boyfriend deserved the most pity.

A warm breeze tousled his black hair and ruffled the collar of his black shirt. His shirt was open to the second button down, revealing his white chest. His sleeves were rolled up to his elbows. His slacks and belt were black. He didn't wear a watch. He probably didn't need one.

He could show up the nattiest of zoot-suited yakuza without meaning to. But Setsura was so handsome that clothes weren't a problem. It was like dressing a sculpture carved by the gods. Their eyes met and the girl's face darkened with unconscious desire. Without knowing it, her lips softened and her eyes smiled.

"If you're waiting for the store to open, it'll be thirty

minutes before my sales girl arrives."

The girl came back to her senses. She blinked her big, round eyes. "Um, my name is Takako Kanan. The bartender told me where to find you. It wasn't exactly *senbei* I was interested in."

"I see." Setsura introduced himself as well. "Then let's go inside and talk it over."

Strangely tense, Takako Kanan stared at the *senbei* and barley tea sitting on the coffee table. She picked up the frosty glass and took a sip.

"It's good," she said with a sigh.

"I'm glad you like it," said Setsura, with an air of personal satisfaction. They were in the tiny, ten-foot-square back office of the Aki Detective Agency (also known by the initials, "DSM"). It was a traditional Japanese room with tatami-mat floors. "So, what did you come here for?"

"There's somebody I need to find."

"And who would that be?"

"A Chinese woman," she said, and Setsura's eyes glowed. Takako didn't notice. "The woman I saw the other night, in Kabuki-cho, around two in the morning. I just have to meet her again."

"If you don't mind, could you tell me why? I can't promise you that I'll take the job, though."

Takako responded with a forceful nod and began to explain.

She lived outside Shinjuku in Hakusan, Bunkyou Ward. She was a college senior, majoring in history. Her specialty was ancient Chinese history. She had tired of book studies and wanted to do more field work. She'd already traveled to China several times, making her fifth trip earlier that year.

She was particularly interested in China's legendary dynastic rulers, particularly the Hsia Dynasty. Since ruins dating to the Hsia Dynasty had been discovered in Henan Province several years ago, a great many new findings had been announced and research papers published.

Chinese research groups were presently in the process of resuming the excavations. However, Takako's research had taken her in a quite different, even radical, direction.

She said fervently, "I want to uncover the truth about Daji."

Setsura recognized the name. Until the discovery of the Hsia, the Shang had been the oldest known Chinese dynasty. Shang had toppled Hsia, in the earliest example of a dynasty founding itself through armed revolution. After six hundred years and twenty-eight successions of power, it crumbled during the reign of Emperor Zhou.

A woman of uncommon evil had led Emperor Zhou to lay waste to six centuries of accumulated wisdom. When he'd conquered the state of Yousu, the daughter of one of the noble families was offered to him as tribute. Her name was Daji.

Practically overnight, in order to win and keep her favor, Zhou turned from an enlightened monarch into a depraved ruler. His tall towers and mighty warehouses bulged with gold and silk and rice and barley and fruit stolen from his subjects. All manner of rare plants and exotic animals were confiscated from their rightful owners and put on display.

In the gardens of gigantic palaces constructed

in Henan Province at great expense and the cost of countless lives, lakes were filled with wine and cuts of fine meat were hung from the trees. His guests—men and women alike—stripped naked and danced through the wooded glens while indulging in every immoral perversion and desire.

It'd be no exaggeration to say that the expression, "To live a life of debauchery" originated with Emperor Zhou.

When the wine turned sour and the meat rotted and everyone had exhausted themselves in violent bouts of sexual competition, bawdy melodies such as "The Northern Town Dance" and "The Seduction Song" would come flitting through the evening air.

As the aroused emperor listened in an ecstatic trance, his poisonously beautiful concubine would whisper in his ear, filling his head with even more temptations.

"*I want to tell a child's sex before it is born*," she'd muse.

And he would respond, "*How would you tell a thing like that*?"

And Daji would say, "*Cut her open.*"

Separated far from the hearts of the people, only the winds of hate and resentment blew down the streets of the capital. Lord Jiu and Lord E, the two advisors of his Executive Council who dared take him to task, were brutally murdered. Those who opposed him were forced to walk across a roaring fire on an oil-coated bronze cylinder.

The screams of the victims as they burned to death echoed alongside any mention of this "trial by fire" unto the end of time.

According to one legend, Daji was a nine-tailed

fox whose soul was the sum total of all the misery and darkness created in the bowels of Hell itself. After the Shang was overthrown by Emperor Wu of the Chou Dynasty, she fled to India. There she gained notoriety as the voluptuous Madame Hua Yang who seduced Crown Prince Banzu.

But her true nature came to light and she fled to Japan. She possessed the body of Tamamo no Mae, the concubine of Emperor Toba, and haunted the Imperial Family until the Court Shaman, Yasunari Abe, exorcised her.

The last days of the fox spirit came in the fall of the year 1137. For two days and two nights, she faced off against fifteen thousand soldiers in a desolate field on the outskirts of Nasu in Shimotsuke Province. Defeated at last, she transformed into a smoldering chunk of noxious lava.

This "death stone" remains there to this day, where the annual Nasu Fire Festival serves to warn of its terrible powers.

Not only the Shang, Takako pointed out, but three ancient Chinese dynasties faced a day of judgment because of this evil consort.

The Hsia Dynasty ended when Emperor Jie was overthrown by Emperor Tang, establishing the Shang Dynasty. The Shang Dynasty ended with the downfall of Emperor Zhou. In the annals of tyrannical rulers, Emperor Jie ranked alongside Emperor Zhou.

Emperor Jie was given a beguiling woman called Moxi from the land of Youshi as tribute. At the end of the Chou Dynasty, Emperor You was served by a sorceress of unknown origins who went by the name of Baosi.

These three courtesans—*sorceresses* might be the better term—were likely all the same person. Several years before the existence of the Hsia Dynasty came to light, portraits of these sorceresses from the Shang and Chou dynasties were unearthed at archeological digs.

They were painted by artists serving in the Imperial Court. The women were identified by name as Daji and Baosi. They looked like identical twins. And despite the faded, scarred canvases, their dazzling beauty and awful wickedness was plain to behold.

Takako naturally jumped at a chance to get access to the Hsia excavations. She had to explore this intersection of history, legend and folklore further. Her uncle was a key player in the Sino-Japanese Cultural Exchange Society. That gave her a lot of pull.

Fifteen hundred feet down, the cold ruins of a Hsia Dynasty palace were unearthed. The complex covered more than a hundred and sixty acres. Responding to her inquiries, an official showed her a bronze mirror. The name "Moxi" was clearly inscribed next to a woman's portrait. Hers was the spitting image of the other women, separated by centuries.

Setsura asked, "So you believe that these three sorceresses are the same as that woman we saw in Kabuki-cho?"

Takako shook her head. "I'm probably mistaken in this regard. I can't believe that the sorceress who toyed with the fates of three dynasties fifteen hundred years ago would show up in present-day Shinjuku. I came here to find examples of spiritual possession and the supernatural. I wasn't necessarily looking for a direct connection to the sorceresses. Short of other undeniable facts, I wouldn't have visited you either. Except there were two portraits etched on the mirror discovered at the Hsia Dynasty dig. Moxi and a younger girl, a maidservant apparently. The same girl I saw on a crowded street in Kabuki-cho."

"That's an impressive memory you've got. Don't get me wrong. I mean it as a compliment."

Takako laughed. "Reserve your compliments for those Hsia Dynasty artists. The French realists had nothing on them. But I couldn't believe my eyes."

"I don't doubt it," Setsura nodded solemnly.

The urgency was there in his voice, and for the first time Takako felt a sense of familiarity with this shudderingly handsome black-clad young man.

"And what were those other undeniable facts?" he asked.

"I started following her. Part of me knew it was a waste of time. She was wearing a *cheongsam* cut all the way up her thigh. She was heading towards Kabuki-cho's *Golden Gai* district. I should have cut my losses there. But curiosity got the better of me, and I walked into the ruins. My intention was to turn around and go back if it looked like I'd be going too far in. We'd come from the street that runs by the ward council offices. She took the first left and I followed her at a safe distance—"

They'd been maybe six feet apart, in the middle of a dark alleyway, when the girl stopped and turned around. The girl looked at her, and Takako felt her blood freeze in her veins. She tried to run.

Crimson flashed in the girl's eyes. As soon as she saw the red glow, Takako felt as if her brain had suddenly instructed her body not to move a muscle. The girl raised her hand, gesturing for Takako to *come here*. Her legs moved of their own accord.

"I was completely helpless. She hadn't said a thing, but my legs obeyed her anyway. I was sure my number was up. *She really is her*, I thought."

"Weren't you frightened?"

"It was more that I was totally spaced out to an uncomfortable degree. My body kept going forward like I was sleepwalking, like my own will was out of my control. It had to be because of those eyes. When I was right in front of her, she stood on her tiptoes and nuzzled my throat. That's when I knew she was a vampire."

"And then what happened?" Setsura asked, eyeing the blue scarf around her neck.

"Nothing. I don't know why, but as soon as her lips touched my throat, she screamed and jumped back from me." Takako paused. "Sorry, it's a little too warm for this."

She unwound the scarf. There wasn't a mark on her unblemished skin.

"Do you know why?"

"Not in the slightest," Takako said, waving her hand. "I took off like a shot. When she jumped back from me, all the feelings returned to my limbs. I ran and didn't look back. Come to think about it, I did hear heavy breathing behind me. Like someone was having a coughing fit."

"Coughing?" Setsura furrowed his brows.

"Hey, you look really cute when you do that."

"Well, ah, thanks. Not to be nosy, but did you have gyoza or Chinese for dinner the night before?"

"No. I had borscht at Nakamura's at the station. Fourteen hundred yen."

"They've raised their prices," Setsura quipped. But he stopped asking about the cause.

At the same time that this Chinese girl was having fits, he couldn't have known that patrol officer Hyuuga

Kaneda had been rendered unconscious in the ruins near Nakai Station, a garlic-soaked handkerchief plastered across his nose and mouth.

“So, what do you think?” Takako asked.

Setsura picked up a thick s*enbei* cracker and took a bite. It made a sharp, crisp sound. Either the loud crunching or the taste made him frown. “Yeah,” he said. “I’ll look into it.”

“Good.”

“But I have conditions.”

“What?” said Takako, unconsciously raising her hand to her chest, as if she expected him to make demands of an untoward nature. But the rapturous echoes in her voice were stronger than the words of protest forming in her mouth. Such was the magic of Setsura’s presence.

“While I’m conducting my investigation, you have to return to the outside world. Don’t ask the reasons. And I won’t ask what you’d do with a girl like that if you did find her.”

“I intend to ask her about her lineage,” Takako immediately answered. “If she’s who I think she is, then this is really serious. She’s not some schoolgirl. She’s a big-time sorceress who brought down three dynasties. Even Shinjuku has good reason to be afraid. I wouldn’t count on the cops or the shamans to get the job done. It’s up to you.”

Setsura smiled thinly. “Because she’s such a dangerous opponent. I can handle her. But not if you’re in the line of fire as well. I don’t admit this very often, but this time around, I’m not sure how things are going to turn out.”

Hearing the ominous undertones in his quick and to-the-point reply, Takako swallowed hard. She said, after a long pause, "It seems you're already onto something. I get it. The word is that Shinjuku's No. 1 P.I. has a well-earned reputation. I promise."

"So you went to the police first?"

"Yeah. But they said all the vampires were living in Toyama, so no problem. Is that true?"

"Not counting *her*, it probably is. As for my fee—"

Setsura picked up his glass. Downing the contents, he let the barley tea seep into his insides as he tried to recall his rate schedule.

That was when the telephone rang.

Chapter Three

The call was from Mephisto. He'd received a message from the Elder of the Toyama vampires. The Elder had woken up long enough to meet with them.

"In the middle of the day?" Setsura practically yelped into the receiver. Ever since those four had arrived, it'd been one weird thing after the other.

He saw Takako off and left the house around ten in the morning. Fortunately, his part-time shop girl arrived as he was pulling on his shoes.

Anyone knowledgeable about the history of public housing in Shinjuku would be familiar with the scale of the buildings in the Toyama housing block and the area they covered. Not only its spaciousness, but the sheer amount of greenery. No matter how blue the skies above, the darkness of the densely wooded areas could easily be mistaken for dusk.

But this was not a neighborhood where couples went for a midday stroll, or children played in the park, or where lines of drying laundry fluttered in the wind. Listen carefully and the growl of distant car engines and the songs of birds grew audible.

A silent place. Tranquility ruled the day. The only humans with a reason to be there were the heavily-armed security guards.

Setsura got out of the taxi. Mephisto and a guard were waiting for him. The man with the moustache wearing a beige uniform was armed with a Winchester self-loading shotgun and a Colt 10 mm Delta Elite with an eight-round magazine. Tear gas and bromide tranquilizer shells were strapped to his belt.

He was one of the guards who watched over this enormous concrete castle during daylight hours. Behind him were high-voltage barricades and armored vehicles bearing the insignia of the security firm.

Setsura quipped, "It all seems way over the top, no matter how many times I see it."

"Hardly anybody's up and about during the day. Just taking the necessary precautions."

With the guard taking point, they passed through the barricade. The gate was operated by another guard inside the perimeter. The quiet descended as they entered the grounds. Setsura hunched his shoulders. Even the temperature dropped.

The guard said, not looking at him, "That's what happens when you pack a couple hundred of 'em together in one place. Been working here for two years, three days on, two off. Still haven't gotten used to it. Any longer and you start getting scared of the sunlight. It's the vibe they put off."

"What the—!"

Several yards ahead, a black shadow crossed in front of them at a blazing speed. It had barely registered to Setsura and Mephisto's eyes as a squat, humanoid figure when a cloud of dust enveloped it. A few tenths of a second later, the roar of a large caliber gun shook the air. The smell of gunpowder stung their nostrils.

The smoke cleared away. With a *whoosh* bright orange flames laced with streaks of soot engulfed the miserable remains. The heat beat against their faces. At its maximum setting, the flame thrower reached six thousand degrees.

"A ghoul," said the guard behind them. "Lately

they've been moving around a lot more during the day. With the vamps all dead to the world when the sun's out, it's a happy hunting ground for the critters. They're like cockroaches. No matter how many you step on, they keep coming back."

"The circle of life," Mephisto countered. "They're just doing what living creatures like them do."

Mephisto's nonchalance rubbed the guard the wrong way. "Beg to differ, Doctor. Nothing about them qualifies as *alive* in my book. Who cares what gave birth to them? They crawl out from under the ruins and sewers at night and feed on rats and bugs. At some point, they started going after corpses and sleeping humans. Count your lucky stars they're not chowing down on normal adults yet. Just babies and the odd senior citizen. They don't touch anything that can fight back. But just when you think they're a bunch of weaklings, you find 'em tossing quarter-ton granite gravestones around like baseballs. They're scaredy-cats, that's what they are. Sneaking around, eating roadkill, screwing and dying—that's all they're good for. What do you think would happen if you took one to your hospital? They'd be having the patients for dessert."

"Oh, I'd kill them before that happened," Mephisto answered serenely.

Setsura raised his brows. The two guards paled a bit—as if imagining that Mephisto's unpredictable sense of judgment might turn on them some day.

"But if they came seeking treatment," the white-clad Doctor of Death continued, "I would welcome them. If the parent of a victimized child tried to exact revenge there, they would have to die too."

"Why's that?" the other guard felt compelled to ask.

"Because that ghoul would be my patient. According to the laws of this city, a cowardly, miserable creature born here has the right to exist here—even if all they do is eat babies. No matter who the patient might be, at my hospital, they will get the care they came for."

"And once it was cured?"

"It'd be promptly killed by the parents of the aforementioned baby. I cannot resurrect the dead. Once the patient has recovered, I can't afford to have them outstaying their welcome."

"You'd save them just to see them killed?"

"That is the law of this city."

The guard pondered that statement.

"When the powers-that-be tried to evict the residents of this housing block, the citizens of the ward signed onto their protection. Because no matter what the form of life, they all have the right to live in this city according to the rules they live by. The only exception comes when *their* lifestyle threatens *your* existence."

Nobody had anything to add to that. They arrived at the steel doors that led into the offices of the building manager. The two-story building covered almost a hundred square yards of ground, but the giant high-rises surrounding it made it look like a dollhouse in comparison.

The guard said, "The Elder is waiting."

Setsura glanced at the front of the building. "The shutters aren't closed, the black drapes aren't drawn. I take it he slept well. That old fart looks to be in as good a mood as ever."

"He must have dreamed good dreams," said Mephisto. He pressed the intercom button next to the door.

"Welcome," rumbled a deeply furrowed voice that

brought to mind the image of an old philosopher bundled up on a winter night, quietly pursuing his theories of everything. "The door is open. Come in."

Mephisto went first, and Setsura followed. The light-filled living room was a good twenty feet long by twenty feet wide. Two people got up from the modern-looking sofa in the center. The smaller of the two approached them.

An old man in a double-breasted white suit. The sunlight slanting through the windows made the top of his magnificently bald head gleam. The Toyama Elder smiled the way any other old man would smile. Setsura said he was a thousand years old. And Mephisto said he slept half the year away.

He shook hands with them, wrinkled hands that contained a surprising strength and vigor. "Welcome, welcome. This is as welcome a surprise as the night coming on. Basking in the honored presence of Mister Setsura Aki and Doctor Mephisto reminds me that no matter how old they may grow, human beings never grow too old."

Setsura looked a bit embarrassed. It was a true enough statement if anybody else had said it, but this old man—

"If Doctor Mephisto felt it necessary to reach out to us, there must be fires in this city that need putting out." The Elder motioned them to the sofa. "If there is anything we can do, we will spare no effort, though I do not think this is a problem that will be disposed of easily. It was enough to wake me from my sleep."

"Enough to—" Mephisto began. Setsura stared thoughtfully at the ceiling. Mephisto finished his thought. "Enough to wake you up?"

Not answering Mephisto's question, the Elder

pointed to the young man in a pale blue suit standing next to the sofa. "Let me introduce my grandson, Yakou. This is Shinjuku's best private detective, Setsura Aki, and Shinjuku's most talented physician, Doctor Mephisto."

"I've heard a great deal about you both," Yakou said, with an elegant but unpretentious bow. More than simple good manners, his etiquette had been acquired over many lifetimes.

"I didn't know you had a grandson," said Mephisto, admiring Yakou's razor-sharp good looks.

"He's been educated in London since soon after he was born. He returned home only six months ago. He's said to resemble myself even more than my own son."

"How about that," said Setsura. This P.I. knew more about the residents of Shinjuku than even Mephisto, and perhaps had a clue or two about what it meant for this old man to so resemble his grandson.

The Elder offered them chairs, and sat back down on the sofa. "The two of you can probably imagine why I invited my grandson to this get-together. The same reason Doctor Mephisto visited the other day and why I willingly woke from my rest. Namely, those foreign vampires—apart from our clans—that have come to Shinjuku."

The old man chattered on like the host of an afternoon tea. In a flash, the room fell into a pensive silence.

"Excuse me, Elder," said Mephisto. "But what manner of nightmare did you dream?"

"Why do you think it was a nightmare?"

"If all we dreamed were pleasant fantasies, we would never wake up. Eight hours in bed would not be enough."

"I have lived for over a thousand years," said the Elder, the emotions rising in his voice. "And yet you easily articulate the truth I have acquired as a result. Exactly how old would you be?"

For a change, it was Setsura casting an intrigued glance at Mephisto. Mephisto didn't answer the question. "As for today's agenda—" he began.

The senior citizen good-naturedly bowed deeply. "I only saw a nightmare, but Yakou had a very different kind of encounter with the real thing. I think you should see for yourselves."

"As you wish," the young man replied crisply.

He went to a door at the back of the room and snapped his fingers, a small but pleasant sound. The door opened. Two middle-aged men appeared wheeling a gurney between them. On top of the gurney was a long, rectangular box. A casket. It shook slightly.

The two men parked the casket in front of the four of them, and left through the same door. Yakou put his hands on the plain, bare cover and effortlessly lifted it open.

"Holy—" Setsura exclaimed, his eyes widening. The strong stench assailed his nose.

The man laid out in the box had both hands pressing outwards against the air, the fingers bent into claws, as if he was about to pounce on somebody. But Setsura and Mephisto's eyes were drawn in particular to the man's police uniform.

"According to our investigation, his name is Michio Hyuuga. He works out of the Waseda station in Shinjuku, and is assigned as a patrol officer to the number two police box in Nakai."

The Elder glanced at his grandson, then refocused his narrow eyes on the gray chest of the dead-looking man. “Before putting him in this coffin, we tried to cross his arms over his chest. This is done in order to contain within the soul any remaining particles of good until the dead cross over the River Styx. But his hands kept returning to this form, his fingers bending like hooks. An animal hungering for blood. The demon my grandson battled last night is unlike any of us. You called shortly thereafter.”

Two pairs of eyes turned with intense interest to Yakou. He nodded, and spent the next ten minutes going over the details of the previous night’s incident.

“So that’s what happened,” Setsura said. His conversation that morning with his new client—Takako Kanan—came together with Officer Hyuuga’s inexplicable assault on a woman he was supposedly helping. “And then consequently—”

“What of the woman?” Mephisto pressed, not giving Setsura time to finish the thought.

Mephisto’s defeat must still weigh heavily on his mind. Setsura did not want to see those chickens coming home to roost right now either, so he let the conversation head off on the tangent Mephisto preferred.

“I got her address and telephone number.” His tone of voice suggested that the two of them had parted ways without pressing the matter further. She was also a resident of Demon City.

Yakou had hauled the officer back here. Before waking him up to begin the questioning, the Elder rose from his slumber. After learning what had happened, he’d instructed Yakou to call Setsura and Mephisto before proceeding further.

“We have ways of making people talk. But when dealing with a mutant strain of vampire, things can get complicated if the initial efforts fail. We thought it wise to call in a couple of experts like yourselves." The Elder grinned.

"We sealed him in this casket with a liberal dose of garlic to keep him under control. Before we proceed with the questioning, though, can you think of any other incidents that might be evidence of their handiwork?"

Setsura started to answer, but Mephisto spoke first. "None at all." Any mention of Hisako Tokoyoda's name would inevitably end up spilling the beans about the fiasco at the hospital.

The Elder nodded. "Fine, then. Let's wake him up."

"Still," Setsura interjected, "it's daytime, and present company excepted, vampires don't go walking around in broad daylight."

"Indeed they do not. Which is why this man should only wake up at night. As for now—" The Elder snapped his fingers.

As if the sun had taken note of the problem and eclipsed itself, the room fell into darkness. Setsura looked toward the windows, at the bright scenery outside. The clear blue sky and the green foliage and the sunlight brimming with life.

But like a landscape painted on a canvas, the light didn't seem to penetrate more than a fraction of an inch into the room. At the same time, the pungent odor polluting the air vanished.

"Ahh—"

A few seconds later, the unmistakable sound of a yawn came from the casket. Officer Hyuuga's eyes flew open. Setsura and Mephisto didn't doubt that true night had suddenly descended.

Another smell rose to Setsura's nose and mouth. The corrupting smell of blood.

The officer grew aware of the four pairs of eyes looking down at him. He smiled. The smile of a carnivore when it encounters a flock of sheep unaware of its true nature. His mouth widened, the pair of tusk-like fangs extended. He gripped the edge of the coffin for support as he slowly sat up. The scars on his neck were gone.

"All right. So who invited me to the party?"

Part Four: Sumptuous Feast

Chapter One

Officer Hyuuga pressed his free hand against his stomach. He didn't appear to be in pain.

"I'm hungry," he said, looking at each of their faces.

The Elder stepped forward. He gestured to Yakou. "I presume that you remember my grandson."

"Oh, yes. I remember very well."

He felt around his windpipe with his left hand. Every word seemed forced out of his lungs by the sheer pressure of the blood and bile within, like a geyser about to erupt.

"You really came to my rescue. Oh, I must thank you for that. Maybe a couple of days in my police box lockup will put the fire back in the belly? Some nightly handiwork with a straight razor. A little here, a little there. Lap up the blood and teach you a good and proper lesson. With guys, you know, the tip of *that.* With girls, it's tits and nipples. Tiny slices. Like scratches. And she's shaking all over. It's the pain, you know, and not knowing what's coming next. Lick it up real gentle-like. Suck at 'em like a baby. Drives 'em crazy. A guy like me sucking up the blood on those sensitive parts. Show 'em the razor again, all shiny and glittery. Maybe down to the arteries this time. Things going *my way* would really help, you know. Plant that thought in her mind and she's lifting up her tits and sticking 'em in my mouth! 'More! More! Please! Suck on me!' "

The man stared up in an ecstatic trance, searching

the faces of the four for signs of sympathy and approval, drunk on his own erotic fantasies.

"A most interesting case," mused Mephisto, staring coolly down at him.

The victim of a true vampire absorbed some of the personality of its sire. The trigger of bloodlust also bared the victim's own animal nature. In that case, the vampire who'd sucked the blood of this police officer was a demon from the depths of perdition. Not a fragment of humanity remained.

"Before taking my grandson to task, there are a few questions I must ask you." The Elder's kindly face did not waver.

"Who is your sire? Where is he hiding?"

"Sire?" Officer Hyuuga glared at the old man. "Nobody like that here. But while we're at it, old man, after your grandkid, you'll do fine. I'm not picky. I'll show you a helluva time. Heaven on Earth."

"If you do not answer the question promptly, I will show you Hell."

Twin flames flickered in the darkness. In the officer's eyes. He leapt from the casket. The black whirlwind in the shape of a human bellowed as it circled the Elder's head.

A scream erupted. The cry spun like a revolving siren and crashed to the floor, writhing and tearing at the dark blue carpet. The Elder raised his right hand and clicked his fingers together. A crisp sound rang out. The darkness lifted and the day appeared.

The whirlwind spinning around on the floor gradually took on the shape and form of Officer Hyuuga. Exposed to the light of day, the freakish twisting of the officer's limbs suddenly stopped. Not because the agony had lessened. But just the opposite. The redoubled agony shooting through his nerves brought every bodily function to a standstill.

The brightness from the windows diffused throughout the room, painting a white spot on the floor.

An inarticulate grunt. A groan. Made by the cop on the floor. The thing that looked like a cop. Rasping and gurgling. What happened next would now and then revisit Setsura in his dreams.

The sound of the mewling officer crawling along the floor. The flesh of his face growing slack and folding under its own weight, gathering wrinkles like skin that soaks too long in a hot bath. And then peeling away. Beneath the peeling skin, slashes like cuts of fresh salmon peeked out. Beads of blood welled up.

The legendary question of what became of a vampire exposed to the sun was being answered in living color.

"What think you? I would assume Mr. Setsura Aki and Doctor Mephisto are used to seeing such spectacles."

Mephisto shook his head. "No, I've never witnessed it before. Haven't had a vampire patient under my microscope. What about you?"

"Who in their right mind would ask me to look for a vampire?" Setsura countered. "I've heard from Shinjuku cops that they burn right up, leaving only the clothing behind. But maybe they're just telling tales out of school. Hey, what's this?"

Officer Hyuuga started to crawl away. This time not motivated by ordinary agony, but with a definite goal in mind—toward the gurney, where a rectangular shadow fell beneath the casket. Bracing his limbs, he moved forward like a climber attacking the vertical face of a mountain wall.

Itsy bitsy spider crawled up the water spout—

Human face, hands and feet attached to a uniformed insect. But with every move he made, the surface of the skin rippled like waves and sloughed off. Where his fingers came into contact with the floor, the flesh crumbled like pastry. And when he exerted himself, dark red pus oozed out from the cracks.

Through it all, the muscles and tendons beneath remained intact. The oozing fluid and rust-red scabs created a grotesque layer of defense.

"It seems that sunlight only dissolves the dermis," Mephisto observed, enormously intrigued. The kind of observation to be expected from a doctor.

"It is slightly different in our case," the Elder said.

Setsura wondered aloud, "So distinctions can be made according to ethnic origins?"

The blood and gore-besmeared demon squirmed at his feet as the conversation continued. The average onlooker might well find their attitude and the dispassionate tones they conversed in even more frightening.

"Very true. Just as distinctions can be made according to blood type. Depending on the race and the life force of the individual, the negative reactions can differ wildly."

"In other words, this one's as tough as a long-lived vampire."

Mephisto shot Setsura a glance. The Elder paid the remark no mind. He reached out and pulled the casket closer to him.

The officer grunted and growled. His resentment was clear in the inarticulate sounds. His fingers had only been inches away from reaching the shade.

"Aargh—" His tongue lolled. He gulped and gasped,

"Help—me—"

His fingers scraped against the floor. The tips of his shoes skidded on the carpet. He barely moved forward an inch. His fingers touched the shadow. The gurney moved again, the same distance he'd covered. The cop had no more energy in him. He stretched out on the floor like an old torn towel.

"Stop—it—help—me—"

His voice hissed out like a small puncture in a tire about to go flat forever.

"Even if he ceases to dissolve, the pain does not?"

The Elder nodded. "There are no further changes to the tissues, but the nerves do not stop responding."

"And what if you threw him out in this condition?"

"He would probably go mad from the pain."

"You don't say," Mephisto remarked in a curious voice. "That is something I would like to see."

"In any case, we must get to the questioning. Please pardon the unpleasantness." The Elder crouched down in front of the cop. "We don't want to go through all this again, do we? But I will not ask a second time after this. Who is your sire and where may we find him?"

The officer contorted his indescribable face. The air escaping from his mouth grated like the breath of a patient on his deathbed. His lips trembled with every gasp. The scabs fell from his face like the petals of a dying flower.

"Can't—tell—you—"

A slight flicker in the expression on Yakou's face caught Setsura's attention.

Stubborn bastard, he was probably thinking.

The Elder rubbed his bald head. "We jumped right to the most effective method, but he is still holding out.

Unavoidable measures must be taken."

Setsura and Mephisto exchanged looks.

Yakou's reply clued them into what he was referring to. "Grandfather, we cannot expropriate his sire's authority."

"I said it was unavoidable."

"Against such an opponent? The people living here are not without other recourses."

"This is only my intuition, but seconds count."

The room grew silent. Setsura Aki and Doctor Mephisto sensed an unspoken dread expanding far beyond the reach of the old man's words.

The cold undercurrents reverberated in his good-natured voice.

"He woke me from my sleep and defied a trial of sunlight. More than our lives are at stake. No, in fact, depending on how this wheel of fate turns—"

He didn't finish the sentence, but his actions did. The Elder reached out and grabbed hold of the officer's hair and wrenched his head back. The bones in his neck creaked ominously. More slabs of skin fell off.

"Whoa—wait a second—"

Setsura hastily interrupted, realizing that the Elder's attention was focused not on the officer's face but on his ravaged neck.

What happened to prey who had already been turned into a vampire being bitten once more? Fear and comprehension played across the officer's face as he realized what was coming.

The Elder's lips touched the raw red flesh of his throat. The officer howled, the roar of a beast. Leaving half of his hair behind in the Elder's fist, he transformed again into a whirlwind and blew through the room.

No one lifted a finger. Not because they didn't

understand what he was up to. But because his flailing about was utterly without reason. The tumbling, spinning, uniformed figure smashed into the wall opposite—and then—it could only be on purpose this time—moved to the left.

"Hey—!"

The officer glowed like a white flare in the direct sunlight from the window. A second later, he flew backwards with tremendous force.

The body lay still at their feet.

"Good job," said Yakou. He'd detected Setsura's filaments coiled around the officer's legs.

"What?" Setsura answered lightly, glancing down at the Elder and Mephisto, who were examining the officer's eyes.

"He's quite insane."

"And that makes him quite useless. We should dispose of him."

"Simple madness can be treated. Our only clue is this policeman."

"This may sound cold, but more such clues will surely be forthcoming." The implications in the Elder's words sent a shiver down the back. "I don't mean to offend the good doctor, but when one of us goes mad, raising the dead would be easier than finding a cure."

The ring on the doctor's left hand glittered. "I won't insist, but how would you dispose of this police officer? Everybody is asleep in Toyama right now."

"The security guards are well-versed in staking techniques. Though they'd be a lot happier doing it to a ghoul."

The Elder snapped his fingers three times. Despite being in a completely airtight concrete structure, the front door opened a second later.

Two guards—different ones from before—stepped in.

"We shall dispose of him according to our methods," the Elder stated in a businesslike manner. He motioned for Setsura and Mephisto to sit down. He nodded his head.

"I'm sorry for creating such an unsightly mess. This is my fault."

"Nonsense," said Setsura, waving his hand. "Who knew he'd try to off himself? His sire has proved as bothersome as any opponent I've faced before."

"And they are likely to feel the same way when they meet you."

"What's that?"

"I had heard the rumors, but this is the first time I have seen Setsura Aki's famous threads in action."

Setsura answered the Elder's praise with an embarrassed chuckle.

"Until he was yanked backwards, I was not aware that they had entwined around him. My grandson is not a man easily taken aback, but even he appears impressed."

"I don't know what to say."

"Providing it was you, I'd happily leave the whole matter in your hands, and entrust as well the fate of those of us who have found here a place where we can live in peace."

"How's that?"

"I consulted with Doctor Mephisto before you came here. The four who arrived in such a strange manner on Fifth Street are at the root of the evil on display. More is to come. As an eyewitness, you alone will know them when you see them."

"Well, one hopes so," Setsura answered vaguely.

He was beginning to guess where the conversation was headed.

"Pardon my forwardness, but I would appreciate it if you would accept this."

The Elder placed a golden card on the coffee table. It was a multipurpose debit card, good for cash, shopping, telephone services, and buying and selling information, as well as for personal identification.

"Last night, soon after waking, I had my bank issue it. It draws on my account. Use it as you see fit. If you will search for those four Chinese."

"You mean you're hiring me?"

"That was the first thing that occurred to me when I woke up."

"Unfortunately," Setsura explained, "I'm here with my client."

The Elder turned to the Doctor.

"So I've been beaten to the punch. But the doctor and I share the same objective. We'll simply split it down the middle. No, I'm not trying to dictate the course you should follow or the methods you should take. Think of that card as a means of guaranteeing your ability to act in whatever manner you see fit."

"A man can't serve two masters. My policy remains first come, first served. Any information concerning those four will go through Doctor Mephisto."

The Elder sighed. "I should have expected as much. Understood. I shall rely instead on the good offices of the doctor and withdraw. But with respect to Yakou, there is one thing I would like to get a consensus on."

Three pairs of eyes focused on the young man standing next to the Elder.

"Some sort of shared connection must have led him to the police officer as well. Yakou should take part in the search. I do not see a downside to the two of you acting together on this. Shinjuku's best manhunter having an extra pair of hands certainly wouldn't impose too heavy a burden?"

"But—"

The taciturn Yakou said, "Though I am new at this, I don't see myself getting in your way."

Setsura shook his head. "Without any experience—"

"I worked as a private investigator in London."

"As an assistant to Sherlock Holmes?" joked Mephisto. "No, sorry. Whether Setsura takes you on as an assistant is up to him. I'm sure he could use the help. I should probably establish a line of credit for him as well."

"Whatever." Setsura added, coolly spurning the offer. "I'm not looking for an assistant right now."

The Elder turned his eyes imploringly toward the heavens.

"That is too bad. If you change your mind, though, let us know. Regardless of the time or place, Yakou will be there."

"I appreciate the offer," Setsura replied graciously. He crossed his legs and laced his hands together on his knee. "What else can you tell us about that gang of four I saw?"

Something glittered in the darkness at the back of his mind, the koto's haunting melody flitting about that beautiful countenance. He could even remember the words.

Crossing the waters we've crossed before
Seeing the flowers we've seen once more

Spring breezes along the riverbank roads
Before we know it, we've made our way home

Changing tack right now might not be a bad idea.

Chapter Two

For the three itinerant workers, the ruins next to Shinanomachi Station on the old Japan Railways line was an ideal location to make a little money. Less than twenty yards from the station, the heaps of bricks and debris left over from the remains of the huge buildings reached out like a mountain range.

Decades had passed since the Devil Quake. Yet everyone who passed close by caught a whiff of the heavy odors whenever the tepid breezes stirred the fetid air. The smell of formaldehyde and many other chemicals of unknown origins persisted as proof of the vast and listless dead entombed in the wreckage beneath the white rays of the sun.

This had once been the grounds of Keio University Hospital and Keio Medical College. When the blueprints for the restoration of Shinjuku were first laid out, the hospital topped the list of structures scheduled for rebuilding. But the tons of rock and concrete remained a graveyard for the numerous bodies buried beneath the rubble.

It was said that the reoccurring paranormal phenomena convinced the planning commission to cease reconstruction.

Structural collapses occurred on a daily basis. Cranes, front loaders and backhoes got away from their operators. The explosives used to break up the larger boulders went off spontaneously. Cave-ins and landslides followed one after the other. When the sun went down, the sounds of countless souls moaning and weeping filled the air.

The reconstruction plans for the hospital were sent back to the drawing boards. Even now, with the noonday sun beating down and not a single sign of life to be seen, the unearthly sensations drifted like foxfire across the hushed wastelands.

The three continued on from the front gate to what had once been the reception area. The "No Trespassing" signs and chain-link fencing had long since been torn down, and crumbled with barely a whimper beneath their heavy work boots.

Despite the devastation, the reconstruction efforts of the Self-Defense Forces had borne some fruit. A passageway the size of a light pickup snaked between the concrete blocks piled on top of one another like abstract sculptures.

Eyewitnesses had reported that after seven at night, a spot of light glowed in the now non-existent waiting room, and a woman in a Japanese kimono could be seen silently pacing the corridors.

But this was a summer morning. Despite the invisible, poisonous currents rising into the air, the sky above was clear and blue, dotted only by the occasional fluffy cloud. From off in the distance came the faint sounds of cars and bus engines.

There were people out there. Living people. A small part of those who otherwise belonged *there* were here as well. That alone provided the moral support these three required.

"What do you think?" The man on the right posed the question to the one in front.

He didn't get an immediate answer. Their "uniform" was a stained T-shirt and torn jeans. Their leader apparently went out of his way to preserve the sweat and grease stains on his, until the cloth had the consistency of leather. From the collar down to the shirttails, not an inch was spared of filth, as if the mutual grime cemented some feeling of solidarity among them.

Rather oddly, the red-shirted leader had his arms extended forward and slanted downward, his eyes half-closed. He flexed his fingers open and closed.

"Well?" he asked the thin man, the one wearing thick, round, wire-rim glasses.

"Well—" How their leader answered depended on who asked the question. His moods changed like the weather.

"Faint, but there's a bunch of responses. And something big here too."

"The kind that'll bring in the big bucks?"

"Hard to tell."

"At least something to match those mouse-sized ones from last time. That'd buy us enough booze to last the week."

The man who'd spoken first had long hair that hung down almost to his butt. "This big this time around." He held his hands a shoulders' width apart. "There's gotta be a shitload in this hospital. We're guaranteed to clean up."

Several seconds passed after the long-haired man stopped talking. The leader came to a halt. He reached out his hands toward a small mountain of rubble on his right.

"There. Behind that."

"Yeah!" the two others responded in hushed voices. They both reached behind their backs to retrieve objects tucked into their belts. The objects snapped into shape as they brought them forward.

Blue-white sparks lit up a yard-wide radius around the long-haired man. He was holding a metal ring a foot in diameter with a one-inch gap in the outer rim. An electric arc jumped the gap. He adjusted the gap to create a crescent-shaped plasma talon that stained the bright daylight red.

The control wires and power cables beneath the talon folded into the collapsible handle of the supercharged cattle prod. Only a foot long, it could be tucked into the belt. The batteries were inside the grip, which was wound with many layers of worn duct tape.

The man wearing the wire-rim glasses was preparing a round tube that looked like a bicycle pump. It had a 30-caliber hole in one end. It wasn't a gun, but the shape suggested a weapon of some sort.

Mouths closed, moving practically on tiptoe, taking in everything around them, the three navigated in formation around the mountain of rubble with practiced steps.

A sound like the peep of a squashed chickadee rang out. Not just one or two. Dozens of chirping mouths called out. Wire Rim swallowed hard. His Adam's apple bounced up and down. His brain was telling him loud and clear that his stomach was way too empty to be attempting this crap.

Leader pressed his back against the uneven surface of the rock pile and craned his head around for a better look. He nodded. That sign of assurance strengthened the resolve of the two behind him.

Leader backed off a step and changed places with Long Hair. Then came Wire Rim's turn. A quick look, and he glanced back at his mates, the elation showing on his shadowed countenance. They'd seen it with their own eyes.

Around the back of the rock pile was a rubble-strewn open area enclosed by three small stony mountains. The jumble of odd-sized boulders strewn across the ground testified to the raw ferocity of Mother Nature's temper. But putting even that to shame was the amazing shape of the open void they formed there.

Jammed into that void were pink lumps mewling at each other with their little mouths. A child would probably call them "rats," and the description wouldn't be far wrong.

Eyes like tiny gems, teeth like gear sprockets protruding from mouths under long snouts. A rat with the face of a ground squirrel.

One was descending to the ground. Six legs moved in mincing steps, heading for the open area. The body was at least a foot and a half long. Armor-like scales covered its head and back, suggesting a prehistoric missing link transported through time to the present.

The gene research once conducted at Keio Medical College had never been in the same league as the Ichigaya Genomic Research Center. But despite the destruction, the experimental facilities and biological samples still remained on the premises. Deep down where backhoes and fiber optic cameras couldn't reach, strange new life forms continued to evolve.

It'd long been a public secret that genetic engineering banned in the outside world had continued inside Shinjuku. Since the Devil Quake, corporate entities with the know-how and the operational scale had disappeared from the scene. For the right price, though, illicit labs and medical institutions elsewhere in the world were happy to take custody of these weird and wonderful creatures.

And in the devastated grounds of Keio University

Hospital and Keio Medical College, these three were happy to hunt down the supply that would meet that demand.

"There's twenty of 'em," Long Hair hissed in an elated voice. "That'll keep us in beer and biscuits for the next three months minimum."

Wire Rim's eyes glittered. "Let's go."

Leader grabbed his elbow.

"What?"

"Make it quick," said the one with the radar-like powers in his hands. "I sense something strange closing in. It's gonna get dicey."

"Got it," said Wire Rim. He shouldered the round tube.

The two stepped out together. Despite having survived on bread and water for the last week, they moved with impressive speed. Before the big rats could turn around, Wire Rim's tube was belching puffs of compressed carbon dioxide.

The glass capsules flew out at three hundred yards per second, struck the rocky mounds and shattered. The liquid inside the capsules vaporized instantly. With a quickness that belied their armored appearance, the rats made for their holes. But the gas caught up with them, like they'd waded into thick mud.

"Hurry!"

Wire Rim grabbed a plastic bag from his pocket. They didn't have the budget for gas masks, so the anesthetics they bought off of black-market doctors dissipated quickly.

Overtaking the struggling rats, Long Hair reached out with his cattle prod. The animals convulsed and toppled over, looking like stuffed animals in a shooting gallery. Biological armor laced with collagen fibers was no better than paper in the face of a two-thousand volt charge.

Long Hair skillfully plucked up the unconscious rats with the metal ring and deposited them in the plastic bag Wire Rim was holding.

"Big catch!" Wire Rim yelled excitedly. "Got more than ten!"

"Yeah!" Long Hair replied, turning around. He froze, his eyes focused above Wire Rim's head.

"What—"

The words died coming out of Wire Rim's mouth.

Even while the impulse to turn in the direction that his partners were looking traveled through his brain, he understood the fate awaiting him and froze.

It came crawling down the rock pile behind him on dozens of tentacles. Each tentacle was no bigger than the lash of a whip. But when the off-white suckers lining the coral red skin attached themselves to Wire Rim's body, their sucking power overwhelmed him and hoisted him into the air.

He screamed and tried to tear himself free. The tentacles pinned his hands against his body.

Dodging the death whips fluttering like a forest of out-of-control flattened garden hoses, Long Hair ran back the way he came. Out of the corner of his eye, he caught sight of the trove of rats being drawn into its clutches.

The vagrants weren't the only ones who depended on them to eke out a living.

This was the cause of all their caution.

"Help! Help me!"

The tentacles spilled out over the rock pile. Soon all

that remained of Wire Rim was his voice and dangling legs.

Long Hair ran as fast as he could. He saw Leader standing in the passageway ahead of him. He looked closer. Two tentacles were wrapped around Leader's neck. Leader grabbed at his throat with his hands. His feet didn't touch the ground.

Long Hair screeched like a throttled cat. He bolted in the opposite direction. The tentacles followed him on the stirred-up currents of air. Off in the distance, he heard Wire Rim's screams and the sound of crunching bones. Now the tentacles were streaming toward him as well.

He gave up and stopped and fell back against the mountain of rocks. By the time he realized that he was leaning back against *nothing*, he had already toppled over into a black hole.

He didn't think about what was waiting for him there. He got groggily to his feet and sprinted away from the danger, deeper into the darkness. He didn't know how wide or how deep it was. He felt the chill of those cold tendrils on the back of his neck. The whipping death tentacles would grab him if he paused for a second. He cried like a baby as he pushed his legs forward.

He was abruptly bathed in light. Sunlight. But there was something different about it. It was a cool, artificial light. He knew he'd barged into a completely different environment. There was greenery all around him. Normal-looking trees and shrubs reached toward the sky.

A long moment passed. He came to his senses and peered behind him. The tentacles had vanished. As had the dark corridor. Trees filled his vision.

Relief battled with a profound sense of unease.

Even in Demon City, paranormal phenomena like this didn't happen to everybody on an everyday basis. If forced to come up with an explanation, he'd say he'd been caught up in a shifting dimensional vortex or had come into contact with a teleportation field that carried him here.

But Long Hair had no idea why.

There was an aroma in the air. The smell of ozone and perfume. He sensed that he was not alone. His ripples of uncertainty grew into waves.

A pleasantly cool breeze wafted through the trees. The sun glittered high up in the heavens. At last he figured out what was wrong. He was surrounded by trees but didn't hear the song of a single bird. Or insect. Not a trace of a living thing.

"What—what the hell is going on?" he wailed.

He looked down at his hands. His right hand still gripped the handle of the cattle prod. He grasped the control and twisted it to the right. The blue electric arc jumped out.

The smooth black bark of the tree trunk next to him belched flame. Purple smoke drifted away on the breeze. He set the current at five thousand volts, more than enough to dispatch any garden-variety animal.

Long Hair finally got his nerves under control. He looked around, trying to figure out where to go next. He heard a sound of splashing water. It came from beyond the canopy of the trees.

He started moving before the exact nature of the sound had registered. His fatigue vanished. He wove through a stand of trees, and another. Surrounded by the unchanging scenery, he lost sense of time and distance.

A bright patch appeared in the woods before him.

Long Hair checked his speed and ducked behind a thicket. He carefully peeked out. Blue water still as a mirror. A small lake. But the sense of privacy—that this all belonged to somebody—chilled his blood.

Somebody else was there.

Or rather, its owner was. There was a young woman in the middle of the lake. Only her head was visible above the surface of the water. Her countenance was quite beautiful. His face reflected in her eyes, eyes that drew him into their black depths.

Transfixed, Long Hair stepped out from the shadow of the trees.

The young woman slowly rose from the water, exposing her shoulders and then her breasts. The clear cascade of water swirled across her generously endowed chest like a glass snake. The bold magnificence of her narrow waist and the lovely lines of her hips must have come into existence when God applied brush to canvas.

Her luxurious black hair coiled around her breasts. She was exposed down to her abdomen, and then all the way down to the dark valley between her legs. But wasn't she in the middle of the lake?

"Welcome," said the girl, now standing *on* the water.

She spoke in Chinese. A native speaker might have recognized the ancient origins of her words.

Staggering forward by his reflexes alone, Long Hair knew that her invitation wasn't for him alone. More men appeared from the surrounding woods. He wasn't the first to be summoned to this world. And they were hard-edged vagabonds like himself.

They looked stoned. In the young woman's searching eyes flickered the fire of prey on the prowl.

Long Hair noticed that all of the men bore small scars on their necks, but his higher reasoning ability had abandoned him the second she had exposed herself to view.

The girl walked lightly across the water, skipping toward the shore shrouded in a miasma of lust. Fish swam beneath the blue surface, but the water only touched the soles of her feet.

She reached the shore and said, without pausing in her stride, “Come with me.”

Chapter Three

The men trailed senselessly after the white, naked body, like a troupe of marionettes jerked along by invisible strings.

They clambered down the trackless path. The thick, tangled roots in their way hardly slowed them down. After ten minutes, they emerged in a garden-like clearing in the woods. The surrounding trees were much lower than those in the towering forest.

Deeper in, directly opposite from where they'd entered, was the first sign of a man-made structure. A soaring rock wall made from rectangular blocks of stone. The wall apparently ran along a long-forgotten boundary line, but the blocks were so tightly stacked together that not even a razor blade would fit between them.

The aura about the place suggested to Long Hair that the wall was as old as the dense, primeval forest. And yet the wall looked as smooth as if the stones had been recently quarried. Time was in chaos here.

He caught an unusual scent in the wind. The smell of cured meat.

"Behold." The girl raised her arms and gestured at the groves around her.

Long Hair and the other men sluggishly looked in the direction she was pointing. Pink lumps wiggled on the branches of the trees over their heads, soft and flabby like gigantic silk worms, or perhaps ox livers with two eyes attached. They clung to the trunks of the trees and squirmed beneath their feet.

Far from finding it all disgusting, the mouths of the vagrants watered like small waterfalls.

The pungent smell stinging their noses came from these creatures. The vagrants looked at the girl, strings of drool hanging from their mouths, knowing that the stink of blood and meat must mask more appealing flavors. Their crazed eyes said that if she tried their patience any further, they'd jump her instead.

She returned their collective gaze with her own look of patronizing disdain, and nodded her chin. The men pounced upon the wallowing, repulsive, squirming creatures.

They became human-shaped monsters and sank their teeth into the marshmallow-like tissues. They tore away at the fleshly substance and gulped it down, savoring the indescribable texture and aroma. They didn't wonder why the creatures didn't budge an inch. Skin and meat gave way with a pleasing resistance in the jaw, but not a drop of blood on the tongue.

The insides were the same as the outsides. The creatures were simply living meat. The sound of biting and chewing and gobbling filled the sunlit air.

"It is called *shirou*," the girl scoffed in a low voice. "*Seeing meat.* Common as dandelions on Kunlun Mountain." She knelt down and picked up a gourd lying in green grass. "This is *huangjiu*, yellow wine."

She removed the small stopper in one end. A mellow bouquet filled the air, the scent of an ancient alcoholic drink. It blended with the smell of the *shirou.* This combination of new aromas brought the men chomping down on the *shirou* to a sudden standstill.

They stared at the gourd in the girl's hand, not bothering to wipe their mouths. A second later they were kicking and pawing at the ground and howling like wild animals.

The gourd sailed out of the girl's hand and landed a dozen yards away in the grass. The men scrambled after it on all fours. The winner of the race grabbed it and filled his mouth from the narrow spout. The rest shoved him aside and struggled for the vegetative vessel.

The muddy booze adhered like glue to their slobbering mouths. A single drop oozing down their throats was enough to send them into a perversely mad frenzy.

They all arose together, dropped their trousers, and stood there proud and tall. All their burning desire was concentrated and congealed in one place. Uninhibited carnality flashed from their eyes, focusing like red-hot laser beams on the grassy spot in front of them.

The girl leaned back, stark naked, against the thick trunk of a mulberry tree. She raised her left knee almost to the vertical. The way she covered her privates and her breasts with her hands smoldered with sensuality.

The black hair pushed up around the hand between her legs. Her other hand pressed firmly against her bountiful breasts. The bud of the nipple poked provocatively between her fingers like a cherry.

But more than that—more than anything else about her—like the rarest of seductresses, the cherubic glow on her face remained fixed in the senses while the supple ripeness of her nude body aroused in men their most carnal desires.

Exposing their lower extremities, they advanced on the female lying there in the grass. The more their foul bodies smoldered with depravity, the more intensely her body responded.

One chewed on her sakura lips. She opened her

mouth, inviting his tongue and fluids. She gurgled and gulped it down. He soon dried out. But others, salivating in torrents like lovestruck dogs, poured more and more down her throat. Until she gagged and the flood spilled out of her mouth.

They attacked her breasts. One suckled the rock-hard nipple of her right. Another tried to stuff his mouth with the hot flesh of her left. Tongues trailed along her belly and thighs, diving into her sex. Mouths nibbled at her toes.

Their copious spittle covered her skin until the body cushioned in the green grass glistened slippery and slimy.

The men knelt in a half-circle around her, their erections sticking out like fat wooden coat hooks. She lunged at the first, taking him into her mouth, lapping and sucking, the wet sounds filling the hushed clearing.

She applied her tongue with a vigorous artistry. The man lasted barely three seconds. He pumped with all his might, filling her mouth. And still had more left to give. She wrung him out, took everything he had, and swallowed every last drop.

The remaining men thrust their hips forward, hope glittering in their eyes.

The girl shifted her position, grabbing the erections on either side of her. The man in the middle moved forward. Working both hands hard, she plunged down on his rod. It looked as if her lips had fused onto his cock.

The man bowed his body back wordlessly, coming and losing his vigor simultaneously. The fluid traced a parabola through the air and splashed against her mouth. The sight pushed the other two to their limits.

The girl anticipated this, tightening her hands and increasing the oscillating action.

Two creamy lines squirted across her throat and right cheek. She let go, panting, and smeared the thick viscous liquid across her face and breasts.

Like they were performing a dance routine, the men turned a hundred and eighty degrees and stuck their stained, ulcerated backsides in her besmeared face. And she commenced licking their asses.

One by one she wrapped her arms around their waists and grabbed their erections. Squeezing and stroking with an unbelievably amorous dexterity, she brought them quickly back to life.

A man circled around behind her and made ready to mount her.

But in the last moment before penetration, a peal of laughter shot through the grove, shattering the mood like a rock thrown through plate glass.

One person there could imagine the face of the woman by the sound of her voice. What manner of portrait would she paint in that moment—a thousand-year-old hag or a matchless beauty with a face to shame an endless field of morning glories?

The girl on the grass dimmed like a fading lamp. The bright laughter robbed her even of her own sense of presence.

The men stared in stupefaction at the source of the laughter, at the top of the rock wall. The woman was bathed in light. Not sunlight but more like the wind fanning an ember into a white hot spark. Whenever a breeze touched her, her body sparkled like gold.

The sight of pure beauty froze them where they stood. Having beheld her, they could never use the word "beauty" to so describe another woman again.

The woman said, "Emperor Jie taught her well back during the Hsia Dynasty. He called it the *Sumptuous Feast.*" She bent her lips into a smile.

According to the tales and rumors that have filtered down through the ages since that time, the Sumptuous Feasts conducted by Emperor Jie featured a pond lined with pure white sand and filled with wine. Around the pond were great platters of meat. Stands of trees were fashioned out of venison and jerky. Three thousand pretty young men and women danced to musical accompaniment.

In the midst of it all, Emperor Jie floated on a boat in the wine lake with Moxi, his favorite concubine, as they indulged their lusts.

But the real repasts that decorated the scene were the *shirou*, the "living food" that drew breath from the earth to constantly regenerate their bodies. And the *huangjiu*, whose intense and unequaled fragrance intoxicated the senses as much as consuming a Yellow River of wine.

And a single girl engaging an army of men with her naked body.

In which case, who was this "beautiful princess," this "Biki" watching so intensely from the wall, her eyes glittering with fire?

A moment later, Biki stood on level ground. She'd stepped off the twenty-foot wall as easily as stepping off a footstool. The apparent weightlessness of her body did not reach the startled thoughts of these men.

Her black hair, combed back and held by a glittering blue sapphire hairpin that amplified its luxuriousness, turned the white rays of the sun to dusk. Her striped, single-layer silk kimono fluttered in the ceaseless breeze. It moved with an airy mesmerizing freedom, maintaining a single, steady rhythm.

Any human being would have felt compelled to bow before the glowing elegance and beauty that was Biki. But only bestial cravings darkened the faces of the befuddled men. Her entire being radiated sexual desire.

With each step, the cut of the kimono revealed the exact outlines of her thighs. The exact shape of her ass. The heft and dimension of her swaying breasts. Every inch covered with cloth, yet the parts taken altogether projected an exact image into the imagination, bringing the men to rigid attention, to the very point of release.

"Shuuran," Biki said. "I haven't seen them before. Did you summon these men here?"

The naked girl called Shuuran kowtowed into the shape of a small rock in the grass. Hammered down and pummeled by forces of a completely different scope and scale, she was reduced to the picture of a cowering, simpering child.

Biki flashed a brilliant smile. "Well, well. In that case, vagrants off the teeming streets of Qin, Zong and Ming. Not to mention Yin and Zhou. But of course, gather them by the thousands and more will find reasons to make merry than to mourn. But so long as Kikiou has his say, their summoning shall be left to him alone."

She paused. "Shuuran, have you received your punishment?"

"Yes." The voice rising from the green grass was no louder than the buzz of a mosquito. "A thousand lashes with a branch of thorns."

Biki glanced down at the girl's unmarred skin. She turned her cold, unforgiving eyes on the men standing there as if rooted to the ground.

"But Kikiou happens not to be in at the moment.

He is a man as faithful to my commands as a horse. He is hunting down the servants that will serve us best, as he should. However, Shuuran, I will remain true to our history, to the ways of life that brought us this far."

The girl's body trembled slightly. She was agreeing with all her might, mind and strength.

"Which is why I cannot allow *this*. Even if I condoned their summoning, I will not allow them to stand before me."

Biki stood before one of the vagrants. Her right hand traced an arc through the air from right to left. At first, it seemed nothing more than a slap on the face. The speed and strength were no more than that.

The man's throat popped like a cork. A *splat* landed on a nearby tree trunk. The man stood there and gawked. He didn't understand what had just happened to him.

Half of his throat had disappeared.

As if finally coming to its senses, the blood gushed into the gaping red hole. The rest of his neck was plastered against the tree trunk. It slid slowly down the bark, leaving a maroon trail behind. The man slowly knelt down along with it. Big tears brimmed up in his eyes. His hands touched his missing throat and he realized what else would soon be leaving him, and he shook his head sadly.

Knowing that this was the end, with a look of resignation on his face, he closed his eyes and toppled over.

The woman watched, then proceeded to the next man. The chunks of flesh disturbed the grass and low-lying branches. Finally, she came to the end of the line.

She faced the long-haired man and looked down

at his right hand. "A newcomer? There are no scars on his neck."

"Yes."

"What is this curious object in his hand? It appears to be a weapon. Shuuran, show me how it works. No. I have a better idea. Try it out on yourself. Couple with this filthy man while you do so. A new kind of intercourse I haven't seen in a while. Here. Now."

"Yes."

An outrageous reply to an outrageous command. But Biki and the girl were connected by the absolute cords of master and servant. Shuuran stood and approached Long Hair with an ease that belied the preceding terrors. Such was the power of any order spoken by Biki.

"Use that thing on me."

The girl spoke in words he couldn't possibly understand, but Long Hair lifted up the cattle prod. He'd abandoned all sense and logic from the moment he'd looked upon her. Now his eyes shone with a terrifying light, filling with animal lusts aroused from the deepest, darkest parts of the instinctual self.

Blue electric sparks jumped between them. The girl writhed in agony. A faint column of purple smoke rose up, along with the smell of scorched skin.

She erased the look of twisted agony and cupped her young, pert breasts. The swell of the left breast was partially blackened like a half moon. The girl's face and chest were covered with semen. A grotesque and titillating sight.

"More—more—this one too." Shuuran pushed forward the unscarred breast. The sultry look on her face arose from the depths of her soul.

Long Hair pressed the button once again.

"Ahh—" she cried, arching her back.

She grabbed his cock with both hands, her body smoldering as she toyed with him. Long Hair thrust his hips forward as he screwed the cattle prod into her chest.

Her breasts melted and incandesced. Yet pleasure twisted her countenance, not pain. She played with his erection with the skill of a virtuoso flutist, the already unbelievable level of her licentiousness only increasing.

The man's mouth dripped as if eyeing a banquet. This squealing girl servicing him was a rare pleasure indeed.

The cattle prod sparked. The fire touched her hips. She moaned. It touched her thighs. She screamed. Her neck sputtered with flames. At last, she pushed her hands back through her hair and turned and gave her sculpted back and tight ass to him.

It was a splendid ass. A delicious ass.

"Hurry—" she panted.

With an indecipherable exclamation, Long Hair jabbed the cattle prod. Her back burst into flames. The muscles of her buttocks popped. A sweet smell arose. Human meat or cattle, it was all the same underneath, and the girl had a nicely marbled flank.

"Ahh—ahh—" Shuuran screamed, shaking her ass.

Her pussy was soaking wet, dripping down onto the grass. With his free hand he grabbed her around the waist and penetrated her, plunging all the way in.

She tightened around him, massaging him inside her. Her muscled walls flexed and twisted, secreting its natural lubricants, with each constriction rubbing and sucking him in deeper.

The man roared, on the verge of coming. But not

yet. He growled and slammed the cattle prod against her back.

The girl's body convulsed and clamped around his erection. Long Hair closed his eyes and ejaculated. It took several long seconds until he was satisfied. Smelling a savory fragrance, Long Hair opened his eyes.

The girl's face was right before his eyes. Shuuran had twisted the upper half of her torso a full ninety degrees. But his mind simply could not seize on the physical incongruity.

She plastered her mouth against his. She really seemed to enjoy it. Her round, wet tongue pushed into his mouth. He sucked on it in a trance. Shuuran pulled her mouth away and bit down on the lobe of his ear. She jabbed her tongue into his grimy ear and puffed hot breaths. Long Hair's body swelled with delight.

Her lips trailed down his neck. There was a short stab of pain and he felt something hard entering him. And then a moment later, something flowing out of him.

"I've seen enough," came Biki's voice. "Finish him off and toss him out with the others. That was a fine show-and-tell."

The voice that echoed in this vagrant's ears meant nothing to him.

Part 5: Bad Seed

Chapter One

Yasukuni Avenue was always thronged with crowds of people shortly before noon.

A tourist might curiously trail after them wondering what the big deal was. Spying the sign on the building drawing them in, "My word," he would exclaim, and then smile knowingly.

The building itself preserved something of an aura from the old days. But that really amounted to nothing more than several aspects of the prior structure being adopted during the reconstruction. The original had been torn down to the foundations.

Employees who'd worked there before claimed that not much had changed about their jobs. The bold calligraphy gracing the large oak sign at the entranceway to the former headquarters of the Pension Fund Association clearly identified its current function:

Shinjuku Ward Government Offices

These days, practically nobody knew why it'd been moved from what had become the grounds of a private hospital to this location.

The staff had been reduced by a third since the Devil Quake. Procedures and paperwork had increased fifty times, but they had three times as many computer installations at their disposal. Thanks to technologies unmatched in the outside world, state-of-the-art biocomputers and light fiber networks had vastly lessened the workload.

In Shinjuku, the words "government work" had ceased to be an object of scorn. But no matter how well they were prepared for the noon break rush, the reception area in the ward office building was packed this day too.

The strangeness began the moment a woman sitting on the sofa next to the window—apparently prompted by the screech of brakes—got up and turned to look at the building directory.

A black curtain enveloped the world.

Backup generators and uninterruptible power supplies were programmed to automatically switch on when power failures interfered with normal work duties.

That didn't happen. Afterward, it was determined that this was because the computers had not interpreted the overwhelming *psychic* force as "darkness." However, at the time, the people in the reception area let their disapproval be heard.

The darkness that surrounded them was total. It was the same darkness experienced inside a coffin or vault, sealed and secured and buried deep within the earth.

The reception area didn't erupt in panic. These were citizens of Shinjuku. A solution or explanation would quickly be forthcoming. As soon as surprise was about to give way to real fear, the darkness vanished, leaving not a single trace behind. As if whatever task had needed doing had been done.

The computers hummed merrily on as they had before. The employees simply picked up where they had left off. None of the usual hitches occurred, such as the date of birth on a birth certificate slipping a day and screwing up the issuance order for insurance cards.

The aforementioned woman—the wife of a respected general contractor who'd been impatiently waiting with a very put-out air—cradled a Persian cat in her arms with greater care than she would ever give her own child. Not a single whisker was out of place.

According to the building directory, the ward mayor's office was on the fourth floor.

The small waiting room off the main hallway was furnished with a desk for his secretary, a plain sofa, and a coffee table.

Mayor Yoshitake Kajiwara was consulting with an old woman. As a personal favor, she wanted first dibs on a shipment of salt from the outside world. When he hesitated, she offered him a sweetener. His big, smug eyes widened even further.

The old woman raised her head. The fierce look on the deeply-wrinkled face—that had otherwise lent her the appearance of a kindly old grandmother—made Kajiwara's whole body stiffen.

"W-What—?"

"We've got guests," said the old woman, her eyes glittering. "And it looks like they're here to make you an offer you can't refuse."

The mayor stood up and started to return to his luxurious desk. All the lights flickered out. A sudden shadow descended upon them. He tried to speak but only babbled in a panic.

"Don't move," the old woman said. The tension in her voice was fused with rapt curiosity.

The mayor couldn't see a thing. He couldn't feel the floor beneath his feet. A primordial sense of unease pressed in on him from the eternal emptiness in all directions. The woman on the sofa a yard away sounded like she was miles off in the distance.

Another voice invaded the darkness; a voice deep, heavy and of an indeterminate age. "I sensed your presence before we arrived. I suspected you would prove troublesome. Nonetheless, I thought it better to seek an audience now. What's your name, decrepit witch?"

The old woman replied, "Don't they teach you manners where you come from, grandpa? This decrepit witch has been walking the earth since there was but one kingdom in the entire world. She will give your memories a good shaking."

Despite the sheer denseness of the blackness, Mayor Kajiwara realized that these other people could see. The hair rose on the back of his neck.

It was silent for several long seconds. Then, "Oh, so the rough work is left to the young?" the old woman said. "I wouldn't want to be in your shoes either. You think this decrepit witch's blood will reward you with a long-awaited stroll in the sun? I don't happen to be in a giving mood."

"Our business wasn't with you in the first place."

The young man's voice pushed the mayor's shock to the limits. The darkness was unsettling enough. These two intruders conversing casually with the old woman only compounded his confusion. The name of his secretary in the next room popped into the mayor's mind.

"Are you there, Oribe? Oribe? Raise the alarm!"

He couldn't tell if he'd gotten through to his secretary, but an abnormality in any of the five basic sensor groups should trigger the automatic warning system. Surely the photovoltaic sensors would be reading off the scale.

"That won't do any good," the old man said.

For the first time, Kajiwara realized that though he spoke Japanese fluently, he had an accent, Chinese or some other Asian tongue.

"Nothing can escape this shadow, neither sound nor light. Nothing that enters leaves. The same holds true for any wired or wireless communication. Mr. Mayor, your secretary is taking a nap. Our business is with you."

"Show me your faces first. Tell me your names."

"You will understand soon. Once you give to us a little bit of what is yours."

"And what would that be?"

"That would be your blood," the old man replied. "However, we must rid ourselves of this annoying woman. We could ignore her and start over from scratch, but I expect she will arouse more of our enemies. We certainly don't need the likes of her as a servant. Only as a sacrifice to our celebration of blood."

Kajiwara still could see nothing. Beyond a few remedial lessons, he'd never been much for sports, let alone the martial arts, and yet even he could feel the bloodlust staining every molecule of the pitch dark. A war was going on right in front of him.

"Stop!" he shouted. He groped in the empty air in front of him. "Stop it!"

Violent psychic waves beat against his face. Sputtering senseless words, he spun around like a top, his body and muscles battling for equilibrium. Other forces controlled him.

Terrifying powers assaulted him, ejecting him from

the black pit. His head struck something hard. He felt like his skull had caved in. He realized he'd landed on the sofa. Either the cushions had turned to stone or his senses were completely scrambled.

The old woman laughed. "Well done for a youngster." This wasn't sarcasm, but the bemused laughter of a warrior who'd found a worthy opponent whose abilities matched her own. "Your *qi* is impressive. But how much have you truly learned in all your young years?"

A bright spot appeared in Kajiwara's ink-stained sight, like a magnifying glass focusing light on a sheet of black paper. The light spread toward the edges of the sheet and the darkness began to crumble.

"Splendid," the younger voice said, clearly impressed.

"You spoke of my country," the older voice said. "Fearful of invaders, my country built walls along the frontiers of the wastelands. In keeping with that tradition, this day we shall withdraw. We have places to go and things to do. But we will return. Witch, I should like to know what you call yourself."

"You tell me yours, and I'll tell you mine."

"I am Kikiou."

"I am Ryuuki."

"My name is hardly worth mentioning, but you would do well to remember Galeen Nuvenberg."

The fissures in the darkness widened. The heaven-kissed light poured down, burning lines in the air. The light struck the mayor's face and scattered like a swarm of fireflies.

The artificial night quickly evaporated. It appeared to Kajiwara's eyes like the last vestiges of the blackness rushed out through the open door.

"My, my," said the old woman, hugging her arms

around her shoulders and drawing a long breath. She turned to Kajiwara. "Are you all right? They didn't come into contact with you anywhere? Your neck in particular?"

"I'm—that's—"

"You're fine." The old woman slowly sank to her knees. "I'm beat. Chilled down to the bones. Here it is the middle of summer and me knocking heads with an unholy crew like that. Incidentally, they nabbed that pretty young secretary of yours on the way out. Listen to me—"

She paused to take a breath, and continued in a steady voice that belied her condition. "Call Doctor Mephisto and Setsura Aki immediately. After that—"

The old woman, Galeen Nuvenberg, the most powerful wizardess in Demon City, suddenly pitched forward with a thump like a withered old tree blown over by a strong gust of wind.

Mayor Kajiwara had crawled back to his desk at about the same time a team of security guards burst in, automatic weapons locked and loaded. For the next ten minutes, the mayor's office looked like a football game crammed into a tennis court.

But even for the mayor of Demon City, Kajiwara kept his wits about him to a remarkable degree.

"I'm fine, I'm fine. Contact Mephisto Hospital and get hold of Setsura Aki. No. Transport this woman there. That's your top priority! On the double!"

He snapped out the orders without a hint of self-doubt. "Ms. Oribe has been kidnapped. Find her!"

That was a grave error.

"After that—" the old wizardess had said before losing consciousness.

If she'd been able to complete the thought, she

would have added, *"When you find Ms. Oribe, detain her on the spot. You absolutely cannot allow her to come into contact with anybody of any importance in Shinjuku."*

Neither did Mayor Kajiwara bring up the matter of his secretary when he finally met with Doctor Mephisto and Setsura Aki. If he could have foreseen the consequences of this mistake, he might well have cursed the day he was born.

In a city already crawling with evil sprites, spirits and demons and all their corrupting vices, the scarlet seeds of a poisonous new weed were implanting themselves throughout its very bloodstream.

Chapter Two

Setsura Aki and Doctor Mephisto politely excused themselves, and left the building manager's office.

A brisk summer breeze seemed to be trying to sweep away the patches of sunlight and shadow. As though shamed by the sight of so much beauty in one place, it could be that the self-conscious wind was simply scurrying to get out of the way.

Such was the striking figure each of these two men cut. The wind furrowed its brows and frowned and turned around and headed in the opposite direction. But the comely countenances of the two men were also tinted by shades of worry that passersby never paused to notice.

Passing through a plaza watched over by a wary armored personnel carrier, Setsura said, "I'm not sure what I was doing there."

Mephisto didn't answer. Not so much because he disagreed, but because he wasn't in an agreeable mood at the moment.

"I'm cancelling our deal from the other night."

"You were the one who brought it up." Mephisto said at length.

"Maybe I did, but that wasn't *me*."

Setsura stared up at a summer sky bright and brimming with life. The only darkness was in the expression on his face.

"Yoshiko Toya is going to tear you a new one."

"Like I care."

They walked on for another few minutes.

"Just kidding," Setsura said.

"I know."

It was an odd conversation, like two friends talking to each other and past each other at the same time.

A burst from an automatic rifle came from their left.

Setsura spun around. A window shattered on the first floor of one of the soaring buildings. A ghoul leapt out, staggered several steps and then collapsed. Blue smoke curled up from the holes in its lumpy, hunched back.

Intrigued, Setsura approached the shattered window. Behind the glass, heavy curtains blocked out the rest of the light. He pushed them aside. There wasn't a small apartment behind the curtains, but a large gray room with the dividing walls knocked down.

Stripped of ornamentation, the bare concrete ceiling and floor made him think of a large hotel lobby after a visit from the wrecking ball.

This was where the Toyama vampires slept the day away.

Cool air nipped at his face and hands. It wasn't air-conditioning. It was the unbreathing presence of the room's inhabitants. The blue faces of the innumerable bodies stacked up in even columns and rows. A few white-haired oldsters. Youngsters in sweats. Golden-haired grannies. Age, sex, nationality—the one thing they all shared was their dental work.

Their fangs.

As soon as the sun set, they would open their lifeless eyes and arise. Quietly exchange greetings, and discuss "breakfast."

"So, how do you think it'll taste today?"

"So, what brand do you think it'll be today?"

Forever discontent with not being able to drink blood the "old-fashioned way," but a civilized vampire had to suck it up and soldier on. That was the bottom line for maintaining this safe place of refuge. There were the girls who showed up at the gates, freely offering to share their blood. But the security guards always gave them the boot.

The Toyama residents sat at the tables in the dining hall and drank from the same tank together. Their own accursed food. The substances that promised them eternal life. The human blood shipped via bloodmobile from the blood bank.

Occasionally a child might offer his throat to his frustrated mother. Or a husband might sink his fangs into his wife's neck. After drinking their fill, some might enjoy each other's company in the upstairs lobby. Others might go for a stroll in the moonlit "dawn" of the night.

Presently, the two hundred or so residents of the Toyama municipal housing project were those full-blooded, legendary creatures of the night. Vampires.

They lived ordinary lives. They worked security at night depositories and twenty-four hour markets, and engaged in other occupations appropriate to their particular talents, and received a fair wage in return. Someone at some point had taken to calling this place a "mausoleum for the sunny at heart."

Setsura let the curtain fall back into place. Even the few faint rays of sunlight had prompted low moans from several of the sleepers in the murky depths of the hall.

"Two hundred, huh?" he muttered to himself.

The fire in the Elder's belly toward their new enemy was because of *them*.

It made sense that the otherworldly atmosphere of Shinjuku attracted vampires like a magnet. Most were refugees and exiles driven out of their home countries by the religious and self-righteous. Like the ancient Jews driven out of Egypt, they had sought for themselves a "promised land."

Still, not to put too fine a point on it, but Shinjuku—where monsters and demons ran rampant—wasn't Shangri-La.

In the beginning, when the whole vampire "issue" first arose, a petition was delivered to the ward government by two thousand signers. It read: "We defend the right of every kind of being (including the supernatural) to live in this city to the best of his or her abilities."

The decisive judgment of the ward authorities to let them in, and sell this abandoned city block to the vampires as a "special housing project" would long be remembered by its inhabitants.

But if the vampires ever came to threaten the "normal" lives of the city's other residents, they were also allowed to take retaliatory measures "to the best of their abilities." If the truce was ever broken, two hundred wooden stakes pounded into two hundred chests at noon would ring down the curtain in half an hour.

A city where life was lived and death was dealt without regrets—that was Demon City.

If that gang of four were "ordinary" vampires, Setsura and Mephisto could sleep soundly at night as well. But the Elder had filled them in on their true natures.

Coldly observing the guards surrounding the

ghoul, with automatic weapons leveled, Setsura asked, "Vampires or ghouls, which is the stronger?"

"Why would anybody need to know?" Mephisto countered. "There seems to be a one-to-one relationship between the two. One of those balance of nature things, perhaps?"

"Perhaps."

The two crossed the compound to the gates. The road continued onto Meiji Dori, where they could catch a taxi. The ruins surrounded them. The sun blazed overhead. It was the kind of place where a person without an umbrella wished for rain.

Setsura stopped. From the top of the gentle hill rising to meet Meiji Dori, an old man dressed in white tottered towards them.

The thick wooden staff clutched in his right hand made him look like an old-time warlock. Setsura recognized him. Did the old man know who he was? He was close enough to make out Setsura's features, but his comical gait didn't change. The eyes centered in his creased face beneath snowy brows narrowed to slits.

A dozen feet away.

Setsura and Mephisto didn't move. Not the slightest touch of stress colored the air. The scene resembled two polite young men on a narrow street yielding the right-of-way to a senior citizen.

Six feet away.

Glancing curiously at the desolation around him, the old man passed by without the slightest reaction, his face completely at peace. As he did, the staff and his right hand waved and vanished in a blur. The crack in the wind came only as the staff stopped moving and returned to its original position.

"Youngsters these days are a violent lot," the old

man lamented. "They'd think nothing of cutting a little old man to pieces. The world is surely coming to an end."

And calmly continued on his way. Setsura softly asked, "You have business more urgent to tend to than me?"

The old man stopped. "I am already late for my next appointment. But I take it you will not let me proceed in peace."

"As soon as you've cut through my threads."

"Today has just been one thing after the next. I really must put my affairs in order. You, man in white, will you be getting involved as well?"

"If you wish," Mephisto said with a bow.

"And seeing from whence you came, then you must know who I am?"

Setsura replied, "Yes. Sir Kikiou."

"Well. You do have the jump on me there. This new city is not so welcoming after all."

Mephisto smiled.

"Do you find that terribly surprising?" His teeth glittered. He was not a man who smiled broadly for no reason at all.

"How much do you know about us?"

"Enough," said Setsura. "You are a Hsia Dynasty warlock and alchemist. Daji, your mistress, is that woman of such malicious beauty. I am less certain about the other two."

"I see."

The old man's staff kicked out like a rearing stallion. Taking into consideration the amazing speed and heft of the wooden staff, it could have crushed a man's ribs like matchsticks.

Except that this man was Setsura Aki. Except that

his opponent was Kikiou. He dodged right, a racing black shadow. But then came a dull thud as if his chest were the skin of a bass drum. Setsura flew backwards a good five yards and hit the road hard enough to dent the surface.

The paved surface of the road. Like it was wet sand.

Kikiou spun around. He furrowed his brows in a glancing expression of admiration. He could tell from the reverberations in his hands. Plastered against the outlines of the human impression in the road was a long black duster.

A whirlwind swept down the street. Kikiou rode it like a kite, spinning into the air and touching down a dozen feet away on the ruins hugging the right side of the street. He perched on the remnants of a rock wall as delicately as a bird, holding on only with his toes. The wall appeared ready to collapse at any second.

He slowly opened his eyes and focused his blazing gaze on his left shoulder, where a large slash divided the fabric. "You cut me," the old man said, impressed. "You cut the robes of Kikiou. What manner of man are you? What manner of city is this?"

"This is Shinjuku." Setsura stood next to the indentation in the pavement. He touched one hand to his chest. "I'm not one for making citizen arrests. Sorry, but I'm going to have to kill you."

That hand didn't require more than a hundredth of a second to shoot out the devil wire. But in that hundredth of a second, his finger froze. A *qi* Setsura had never experienced before erupted from Kikiou's cuffs and from beneath the hems of his robe.

"Come," the old man said, beckoning to him with a hand that looked like a piece of weathered wood. "Come into my fold, where my lovely sheep are waiting for you."

A shadow fell across the sun. The dense, eerie vibe excited even the atoms in the air. Setsura and Mephisto couldn't easily break through it.

"Oh, you're not coming? If you do not, I shall take my leave. To a place that you will never find."

He smiled invitingly, the way a spider smiles at a fly. Setsura stepped forward. He didn't look at Mephisto. Mephisto wasn't playing follow the leader. That wasn't the way the two of them worked.

The psychic field enveloped him. Setsura heard a strange sound. The sound of a heavy revolving thing. A number of them. The sound came from beneath Kikiou's clothing.

The pile of bricks swayed. *Something* pushed up at them from below. In the next moment, it reached maximum force and struck in a surging blow.

The bricks went flying. And that *something* rained down. Each twenty inches long and weighing six or seven pounds. Setsura quickly recognized them. Dozens of pink, naked babies.

"Can you kill them?" Kikiou asked. His unearthly *qi* smoldered like heat waves. "Kill something with a baby's face and body? I'm sure *you* can."

He pointed at Setsura. The message was clear. Setsura's devil wire would cut their throats like a hot knife through soft butter. The babies scrambled toward him at an inhuman speed. For some perverse reason, the tottering figures retained all of an infant's cherubic innocence.

Setsura spun the devil wire as he backed up, ensnaring the soft, pink skin. Given his abilities, that should have been sufficient to check their forward progress. But their hands and necks spouted blood.

Heartrending wails burst forth. A slight agitation arose in Setsura's actions. The pink blobs fastened themselves to his shoulders and ankles and sank their teeth into his flesh.

The skull-piercing pain was enough to drive the bravest man momentarily insane. It diminished and then vanished. The ghastly children clutched their hands to their severed faces as they tumbled to the ground. They hadn't seen the web of steel the *senbei* shop owner had wound around himself.

The babies stopped springing upon him, and looked up at him. The angelic countenances flickered only momentarily, revealing their true demonic forms. It was a monumental error on their part.

Before they could again put on their childlike masks, their little heads went flying. And what gushed out of their necks was not blood but dark blue fluid.

Setsura retreated. He could already sense Kikiou on the move. He glanced back. The murderous *qi* exploded around them. Setsura spotted Mephisto's white-clad form on the road ahead.

The demon children dissolved into blue-black pools. In a few seconds the wind would sweep away the toxic miasma.

"What?" Setsura asked.

Mephisto held up his right hand. The thick shard of a needle jutted out from between his thumb and forefinger. One edge glittered like it had been severed with a knife. Setsura's eyes brimmed with curiosity, wondering what fighting style it revealed.

"So you're letting him get away?" he asked, a touch of sarcasm in his voice.

"Whatever cutting I intended to do, I ended up

being cut instead. He's not flesh and blood." Mephisto looked at the street and then at Setsura's shoulder. "You don't want that poison circulating through your veins. We should open it up and burn it out."

"I'll take care of that myself, if you don't mind."

Setsura coughed. The result of the first blow Kikiou had delivered with his staff.

"That is some *qi*," Mephisto diagnosed. "It messed up my aim as well. I haven't seen skills like that in a long time."

"China's a big place. And we're talking about *them*."

Mephisto nodded. "I sensed a touch of fatigue. He wasn't at full strength."

Which meant that this old man at half his powers had escaped death or capture at the hands of Doctor Mephisto and Setsura Aki. The Demon Physician and this demon-haunted *senbei* shop owner looked back at the place they'd come from. Kikiou was headed in that direction.

Setsura mused, "I wonder if he was going to see the Elder."

Mephisto didn't disagree. "I thought they might lay low until they got acclimated to the environment. That doesn't seem to be the case. They're quick studies. They must have put their time in exile to good use learning the ways of the modern world."

"We should make sure the Elder has got the protection he needs. Our strongest ally right now is his gray matter. We wouldn't want anything funny happening to it."

"What kind of protection would actually do any good?"

"How about a bunch of four-leaf clovers?"

"Besides that." A strange light burned in Mephisto's eyes.

They silently gazed at the corner on Meiji Dori. The Elder had a good deal on his plate. And if *they* could sniff out the Elder's home turf in only a few days, they'd have no trouble finding a certain hospital and *senbei* shop.

As for Setsura Aki and Doctor Mephisto—who in this city would be willing to sign up to bodyguard them?

Chapter Three

There were three types of souvenirs that tourists visiting Shinjuku never left without:

1. Fashion accessories (made from demon teeth or claws).
2. Amulet and incense sets (for exorcising ghosts).
3. Plasmodial slime monster globes (non-toxic species).

To be sure, these were really the three runners-up. The three souvenirs that people *really* wanted were illegal in the outside world:

1. Shinjuku spirits (of the highly distilled sort).
2. Divining rods (for casting death spells).
3. Demon extermination kits (including poison).

Nevertheless, Shinjuku's "exports" caused no end of problems in the outside world.

A subdivision in Negishi was reduced to skeletal remains as *Kuronami* spiders multiplied in number to ten of thousands in a single night, and swept through the neighborhood.

One morning, a VP in line for the top job at a certain corporation drowned in his car on the way to work. It could only have been the work of a Shinjuku shaman employing a highly-localized hypnotic spell.

Despite the best efforts of the Shinjuku police, perils that could only have arisen in Demon City crossed the borders, leading to all kinds of gruesome "accidents." It was also a simple fact that there was no shortage of traders and buyers willing to deal in exactly those "products."

Like Chinese restaurants and convenience stores, "antique" and "souvenir" and "curiosity" shops hung out their shingles everywhere in Shinjuku.

A little past two in the afternoon, Takako Kanan pushed through the bulletproof glass doors of Takada no Baba, one such famous "specialty store."

"Welcome," came the owner's voice from the glass-walled enclosure in the dimly-lit rear of the store. He had a head of hair like an exploding mop. A black patch covered his left eye.

Takako wasn't at all cowed by his appearance. She nodded and glanced around the store. Though it looked like a cramped, one-story shop from the outside, the inside proved impressively expansive. There was another door to the rear of the glass enclosure, and more rooms deeper in.

U.S. military and Japan Self-Defense Forces bomber jackets and uniforms hung on the walls, along with flak jackets, body armor, and strength extenders. Hand-to-hand combat accessories, old-fashioned bazookas and flame throwers, high-powered lasers and much more were all randomly crammed together.

One look at the owner's face said that he'd happily supply the (illegal) ammunition as well. This was a small sampling of the "merchandise" that "souvenir" shops typically handled, not to mention a few other oddities scattered around the shop:

— A fetus with two heads squired in an artificial womb filled with amniotic fluid.

— A figure of a lizard demon sealed inside a building cornerstone dating back to the Showa Era.

— Yellow tentacles oozing out of the mouth of a bottle stoppered with a heavy concrete block.

— The strangely-shaped leaves of a bizarre, cactus-like plant moving in synchronicity with the yellow tentacles.

— A French doll gnashing his jaws, its sharp upper and lower fangs clicking together.

— A shady-looking face continuously emerging from a smoldering haze in the glass of a hand mirror.

— A woman's arm severed at the shoulder dragging its ball and chain across the floor, searching for what had held it in a stranglehold.

If you really want to know Shinjuku, the word on the street was, *you have to come here.* Veteran sightseers, underworld types and black marketeers knew that this was the place to get everything they needed.

For that reason alone, the one-eyed proprietor viewed a college student like Takako with undisguised suspicion and annoyance.

"No, you don't," Takako scolded, deftly pirouetting out of the way as the arm made a grab for her ankles. She looked here and there, when suddenly her big brown eyes focused on one specific object.

A big black lump sitting next to the dusty showcases.

She hurried over to it, her face bright with curiosity. It was a strange thing indeed. The shape suggested a giant black peapod about six feet long and a yard in diameter in the middle.

The top half was propped up with a bloodstained iron rod, so it must have some weight and heft. A sack of its size could comfortably hold the average human being. That left the question of what it was made from.

There wasn't any luster to the surface, which didn't have any bumps or divots. It wasn't made out of cloth or metal.

Takako picked up a piece of glass from the top of the display case (labeled: "Mitsukoshi Department Store window glass, destroyed in the "Devil Quake") and tossed it at the black thing.

The "peapod" absorbed the shard without any sign of resistance, without a wrinkle in its skin.

"You owe me for that," the proprietor said bluntly.

Takako asked, "Where did you find it?"

The proprietor simply folded his arms. Takako took a small purse from the breast pocket of her jacket. "Five thousand yen."

"Ten," was his counter offer.

"Seven."

"It was discovered in the middle of the afternoon at the ruins of the Mt. Tenjin amusement park. A kid threw a rock at it."

"And it got sucked up?"

"No, the thing tossed it back. I had it hauled back here. That's the first time I've seen it do that."

Takako leaned over.

"Whoa there!" said the proprietor, but the words had scarcely left his mouth before Takako had thrust her pretty face against the side of the mysterious sack.

She closed her eyes just before impact. The feeling of having penetrated the surface came not from any sense on the skin, but when all the sounds around her grew muffled.

She steeled herself and opened her eyes, but couldn't see a thing. Only darkness. A cold tendril of fear—the dread of being trapped in here forever—touched the back of her neck. It seemed a much larger space inside than out. There must be all kinds of junk lying around in there.

A small moan of terror escaped her lips. Takako pulled back, to where normal light and sound awaited her.

"How much for this shadow box?"

"Hard to say." The look of the shrewd bargainer rose to the proprietor's face. "It's the most popular item I have in stock right now. Five hundred grand."

"You expect a college student to afford that?"

"You're welcome to stop in anytime. There's plenty of buyers in this city."

"Yeah, I know," said Takako, raising the stakes as well.

She tore her gaze away, and looked instead at the cases lining the walls. It wasn't easy to pretend indifference. She wasn't sure she could pull it off. She couldn't read his face. She thought of bidding him a good day, while giving herself enough of a look to gauge his expression. But that would mean showing her hand.

Her heart pounded in her chest. She had only one deal of the cards. Carrying herself as nonchalantly as possible, she headed for the exit. She put her hand on the brass handle. *Damn*, she thought to herself.

Something soft wriggled against her palm. The head of a snake reared up from the handle and flicked its red tongue.

"Hey!" she yelped, jumping back several feet.

Behind her, the conniving voice of the proprietor said, "For a cheeky lass like you—two hundred grand. I can even arrange for installment payments."

The door handle returned to its inorganic form. Takako took a deep breath and nodded. Her beating heart calmed down. The proprietor looked on with cool eyes as she returned to the display case and got out her checkbook.

"So, how do you plan on moving it?" he asked unhelpfully.

"I'll call a taxi. Can I borrow your phone?"

"Taking it outside the ward?"

"No."

"In that case, I'll deliver it myself. For free."

"That's okay," Takako said.

The smile didn't disappear from her face. The proprietor impassively reached for the phone behind the counter.

Thirty or so minutes later, the taxi stopped in front of a *senbei* shop in West Shinjuku. The driver helped get the package out of the back seat. Takako pushed the button for the Aki Detective Agency intercom. The shop girl emerged to say that he was out. He'd been home earlier but had been called away on an emergency.

Takako asked if she could wait, to which the shop girl agreed.

"Sorry to impose, but could you help me haul this thing inside?" She indicated the strange-looking package.

The shop girl frowned. Takako suggested that the concrete-lined storage alcove adjoining the small back office would be fine, and she relented.

The thing weighed as much as the average adult man. Lugging it through the doors, Takako glanced nervously at the sky. The white sunlight was growing listless and thin. It was three hours to dusk. Then came the Demon City night.

Setsura had received a phone call from Mephisto. Galeen Nuvenberg had arrived at his hospital in critical condition. That was startling enough. The fact that the mayor had escorted her there made it all the more so. And when Setsura learned the facts of the case, they were downright astounding.

The special containment ward in the fourth basement level. Naturally, she was being attended to by the hospital director himself and the nursing chief of staff.

Hearing the details from the mayor, Setsura glanced at Mephisto, standing like a statue next to the bed. No words were spoken. Everything that needed saying at the moment could be said with the eyes and under the breath.

— The timeline suggests that Kikiou headed toward Toyama after leaving the mayor's office.

So it seems. For the time being they must be refining their tactics.

— They didn't think twice about mixing it up with the top brass in the ward, and then start dispensing with the competition. That puts us in a dicey position.

We'd better watch our health. Now we're a woman down.

— Kikiou can walk around in broad daylight. When it came to invading the mayor's office, he could have waltzed right in. The darkness must have been for his younger companion, the one called Ryuuki.

In other words, we tangled with a "normal" human, gave only as good as we got, and let him get away. I say, mum's the word on that one too.

— Then where did he go? Taking on the Toyama Elder would require full fighting strength. He was apparently in good shape leaving the mayor's office. But maybe they didn't come away unscathed and had to find someplace to lie low.

Maybe. Sounds like something more in your job description.

The implication being that he wasn't getting the job done. Setsura shrugged.

The mayor cleared his throat. "Would you have any idea what Galeen Nuvenberg wished to speak with you two about?"

Sensing that the mayor was aware he'd been saved by a person with more than mere paranormal abilities, Setsura asked, "You mean, knowing who she is and all?"

"I've heard she was the Czech Republic's greatest—and for a thousand years its only—wizardess."

Setsura smiled thinly. He would have expected the three-term mayor of Demon City to be something more than a run-of-the-mill party hack. And indeed, all the evidence Setsura had seen suggested that the mayor was a real political operator. Except that the biggest wheeler and dealer in Shinjuku, with eyes and ears everywhere, now had a fearful look in his eyes.

"It's a mystery to us as well," Mephisto answered. "But we can hazard a guess."

"Oh?"

"The master of the darkness that visited you was a vampire, and a powerful one at that."

"What?" exclaimed Mayor Kajiwara, though the expression on his face barely flickered.

Only those in the outside world had any right to express real surprise at the mention of "vampires" and "ghouls."

"We are not certain where they came from, but it is a gang of four, and we have confirmed the identity of two of them."

"And they are?" Kajiwara leaned forward, his eyes brightening.

"One is the infamous Daji from ancient China. The other is an old man by the name of Kikiou, the most accomplished warlock of the legendary Hsia Dynasty. They are both over two thousand years old. In fact, it is likely that Daji was born before then. The other man and woman remain mysteries. According to the Toyama Elder, they've popped up here and there throughout history, and not just in China. The last place Daji and Kikiou were observed by themselves was in Northern India during the first century. The four were seen together in the city of Lajia on Mt. Anyemaqen in the year 401."

Doctor Mephisto paused to point out that the other two must have joined them sometime between the first and fifth centuries.

"They showed up a thousand years later during the Saint Bartholomew's Day Massacre in 1572. And then disappeared from the history books. The Elder hypothesizes that they looked into the future and foresaw the emergence of a city that would fit their needs perfectly. So they hid themselves away in a dimensional void in preparation for that day."

"And now they have emerged—"

In response to Kajiwara's statement of the obvious, everybody present felt a lurch in his chest, as when a roller coaster reached the peak of its climb and started to descend.

"—having completed all their preparations," Mephisto replied, in a tone of icy, academic indifference.

The mayor's composure broke there for a moment, but his customary matter-of-fact expression soon returned. He said in an equally unruffled manner, "Considering what has happened of late, I'm inclined to believe the arguments you are putting forth. What powers do these beings possess?"

"Possibly more than our own."

Kajiwara fell silent, waiting for Setsura to object to that assessment. Setsura didn't. "What is their objective?"

"The subjugation of this city. And turning the powers-that-be into their puppets by turning them into vampires."

Mephisto relayed the ghastly truth with the clarity

of a note played by a maestro. That was enough to send chills down the spine.

"Perhaps Miss Nuvenberg sensed their true nature and intended to communicate it to us. Vampires are unrivaled in the dark, while the day turns them into sitting ducks. That means they have to keep themselves hidden at all costs. Throughout the broad sweep of history, no one has uncovered their hidden sepulchres. But this city—"

Kajiwara looked at Setsura, his eyes filled with infinite confidence.

"—this city has Setsura Aki."

"Exactly."

"And Doctor Mephisto."

"Much obliged."

"You mentioned that you met with the Toyama Elder. Is there any possibility that these vampires belong to any of their clans?"

"Trust me when I say that there is not."

"Huh." Suspicious of everything, he didn't say that he did or didn't. That was to be expected of the mayor of Demon City Shinjuku.

"The latest incident has the Elder all the more concerned," Setsura continued. "Rampaging vampires put their own safety and peace of mind at risk. Enraged citizens are liable to break out the stakes and mallets and violate their resting places. Done under the shining sun, they wouldn't have any viable recourses."

"Ah."

Mephisto added, looking down at Galeen Nuvenberg's drawn cheeks, "With their welfare in mind, I would ask that you keep any possible countermeasures tightly under wraps."

"Would measures equally effective against the

Toyama vampires be acceptable?" Kajiwara asked imploringly.

It was all a front. He revealed weakness only in order to maximize sympathy and cooperation for his personal goals. Even knowing that, his opponents couldn't help but fall into the trap. That was the kind of man who lived inside the facade of this virtuous leader of men.

"For the time being," Mephisto conceded. "However, the only reason you are here with us now is because this old woman was there with you. Shinjuku's movers and shakers won't be so fortunate as to have the protection of the Czech Republic's greatest wizardess."

"Then what should we do?"

"I shall leave it to Aki-san to uncover their hiding place. Starting tonight, all important bureaucrats and politicians should be kept in undisclosed locations from sunset to sunrise. They should be driven by trusted drivers and accompanied by trusted bodyguards. The services of a powerful psychic would be a useful backup, but not necessarily. By the time they were detected, the game would be up anyway. Until this matter is resolved, they cannot tell anyone—including their families—where they are. All communications should take place over secured lines."

"Just a minute," Kajiwara said, holding up a hand. "Are all these steps really necessary? Once these vampires have quenched their thirsts, won't they just calm down and move on? Why would they care what position the victim holds?"

"That's why we're confining ourselves to the big shots. Right now, nobody knows what these new vampires are planning. Miss Nuvenberg apparently has an idea, but there's no asking her now."

"And *Doctor Mephisto* can't do anything about that?"

Kajiwara emphasized the name of the Demon Physician. It wasn't clear whether he'd done so on purpose. If he had, then it was likely unconscious. The product of his naturally calculating impulses.

"Unfortunately, as things stand now—"

"—you're not holding out a lot of hope."

Kajiwara's shoulders drooped. He looked like a middle-aged man who'd lost his family and his fortune and teetered on the edge of self-destruction. It was an expression of dejection that prompted bystanders to step forward and take up the reins.

"But there are steps we can take."

Doctor Mephisto spoke crisply. He didn't intend his cool exterior to be encouraging. It was his natural ruthlessness. The mayor's stratagems didn't work on them.

"Yes, exactly." Kajiwara raised his head. He looked resigned to the course of action. He said, filling his voice with determination, "We must strike while the iron is hot. But without divulging anything. I definitely want to have you two as part of my brain trust. Here, wear these—"

He produced two golden badges from the pocket of his suit coat. A child would recognize them. They identified the mayor's Special Investigations Unit. They weren't handed out willy-nilly, but put one on, and doors would open up right and left.

Access to the best restaurants and hotels. Free fare on any mode of transportation, public or private. It bestowed the authority of a police detective, and the right to order beat cops around at will. No one was surprised when a yakuza dealing knock-off badges on the sly was gunned down by his own *oyaji* in a public eatery.

"Sorry," said Setsura Aki, and he really did sound sorry.

"The body count is high enough already," said Doctor Mephisto, as if seriously questioning the man's sanity.

"I see. Well, I'm not surprised. However, Aki-kun, if what you are saying is true, the fate of Shinjuku hangs in the balance. I must know everything about these new vampires as soon as you do. My private line is 011111. I'll give you all the support I can muster."

"Understood, Mr. Mayor."

"And we shall leave it at that. Let's be sure to keep today's conversation between the three of us."

After the mayor left the room in a hurry, Setsura examined the backrest of the chair he'd been sitting in and plucked out a small shard of metal.

"It's a bug. He's as two-faced as they come. But don't worry. He seems to know what he's doing."

"One hopes." Mephisto's voice was as calm as ever. "And whose side are you on?"

"Whose side do you think?"

"Don't take it personally."

"Or I'll lose my head too?"

"Well—"

"Ask me again when I am *me*."

The conversation was going nowhere. Setsura turned his attention to Galeen Nuvenberg, lying on the bed. "So, you really can't do anything about this?"

"I am getting a fundamentally different vibe than what you experienced. As if that *ether* that constitutes the very wellspring of life has been ripped out by the roots. I've done all that I can, but recovery will take some time."

"You're not holding out a lot of hope."

"The mayor can do without the two of us. Everything depends on what you can turn up. We don't know what those vampires have in mind for this city, but the faster we find out where they are hiding, the better."

"Aye, aye." Setsura turned and headed to the door. Then he stopped and said mostly to himself, "Five o'clock? That's when the lights come on. The artificial light drives out the natural. It creates its own kind of darkness."

Sitting in the back room of Aki Senbei/Aki Detective Agency, Takako fought off the anxiety welling up inside her. She was still okay. The lights were still on. She could still hear the voices of people out front. The shop girl was still at work. The tea was getting cold. It was about time for the shop girl to check up on her and get her a refill.

At some point, Takako became aware of her attention drifting back to the storage alcove. She hastily refocused her eyes on the teacup in front of her. Come to think of it, she was looking at it an awful lot. As dusk grew closer, that's where her attention was drawn. She should have left it back at the shop.

The contents of the shadow box emerged at sunset, the shadows within that provided protection from the rays of the sun dissolving into the dark night. The mad alchemist Kikiou had made it under orders from Daji, that Hsia Dynasty witch and seductress. A box of artificial night for those creatures that could live only in the dark.

In the harsh sunlight at the amusement park, it

had repelled stones thrown at it. In the dim light of the curio shop, the tension in its skin had relaxed, allowing a thrown piece of glass to penetrate it. Takako had deduced from its properties what it was. Her great delight was soon tempered by the realization that the only person capable of confronting what was inside the shadow box had still not arrived.

By the same token, though, it wouldn't matter now where she took the thing—if what she *imagined* was inside the shadow box really *was* inside it—

They would notice. And see. The dimly-lit concrete floor of the storage alcove.

Dim? The light wasn't on. With a shudder of fear, like being doused with a bucket of cold water, Takako got unsteadily to her feet and felt around the wall in the *genkan* until she found the switch.

The electric lights were bright. Brighter than the light outside. She breathed a sigh of relief. Only to realize that she was just as nervous as before.

Why did she continue to stare at the light switch? Why didn't she turn around? Why didn't she *want* to turn around?

She heard a sound behind her. The sound came from the storage alcove. From where the shadow box sat on the concrete floor.

She caught her breath.

"That was an eventful ride," a man's voice said. "I seem to have been transported to another place. Woman—where am I?"

She must not answer. She must warn the shop girl. She must—But she found herself saying smoothly and without hesitation, "Aki Senbei, in West Shinjuku."

A short silence. Then the voice filled with an indescribably eerie and unearthly joy.

"One unlikely encounter after the next. I had intended to come here after visiting Toyama. And where may I find this Setsura Aki?"

Part 6:
Beautiful Obsession

Chapter One

A new patient arrived at Mephisto Hospital thirty minutes after Setsura left. It was almost six o'clock. The diluted shades of gray along the dusky streets were growing deeper.

Identifying the visitor on the monitor, Mephisto brushed the black locks from his cheeks. No matter what expression he wore on his maddeningly attractive face, its sheer beauty alone seemed to render it as expressionless as an ancient marble statue.

But this expression showed a rare difference. Though exactly what kind of difference was hard to say.

Several minutes later, Yakou, the grandson of the Toyama Elder, appeared in the doorway of his personal examination room. On the gurney, wheeled along by three men, was a black lacquer casket. Their lineage was obvious from their pale, bluish skin and red lips.

Only Yakou entered the room. "You wouldn't perhaps be the patient?" Mephisto asked.

The typical patient would have practically swooned at the question. Yakou only shook his head. "I wouldn't mind if it came to that, but this evening I am accompanying the patient. He is in here."

Mephisto shifted his attention to the casket. "Somebody I know?"

"The mad police officer. Grandfather asked me to dispose of him. I chose to hand him over to your care."

"A wise decision."

"Thank you." Yakou nodded. He didn't look directly at Mephisto. Even the grandson of the Elder was not immune to the doctor's unrelenting charms.

"I may restore him to sanity, but making him see the light, so to speak, will be up to you."

"I understand. So you will give it your best shot."

"That would be one way to put it. That sire expropriation technique should come in useful."

"I am in no way my grandfather's equal."

Mephisto seemed to have grasped something of what that meant in the meantime. "I understand. Let's open it."

Yakou turned to the casket and tapped lightly on the paneling. The casket was six and a half feet long, two feet wide and two feet deep. The heads of the nails holding it closed were visible.

Without the sound of any of the nails extracting themselves from the wood, the tapping somehow released them. The paneling opened like a Chinese puzzle box, as if some delicate balance had been tipped. It was a nice trick.

The smell of twisted entrails filled the room. A decaying, rotten smell. The air filtration system started up somewhere in the background, replacing the stench with a scrubbed, aromatic scent.

The uniformed mass of flesh scorched by the sun had continued to putrefy. Apparently unperturbed by evidence of microbiotic processes at work on this unmoving, unbreathing blob, Mephisto asked Yakou, "Will these sunburns heal?"

"After a long time and if confined to the dark. A complete recovery is unlikely, but the wounds will heal for the most part."

Mephisto asked under his breath, "The question

is, will the soul heal as well?"

Yakou said encouragingly, "I would bet on the Demon Physician."

"That's right."

Yakou retreated toward the window. Observing him out of the corner of his eye, Doctor Mephisto approached the gurney. He'd taken several steps when the disassembled panels reversed themselves, reassembling the casket in the blink of an eye.

"Well!" Mephisto remarked with great curiosity. His eyes narrowed. "I've never seen such a thing before. Is it common in your world?"

"No," Yakou said with a thin smile. "It's from Su Prefecture in China, a product of the Song Dynasty. It looks like it's frightened of you, Doctor."

"A doctor cannot truly treat a patient who doesn't trust him. Perhaps we should change physicians."

"I don't think that would be good for the patient."

"Then I must try to make myself more likable."

Yakou wasn't sure how to interpret this remark. It wouldn't be an unusual statement from an ordinary doctor. But Doctor Mephisto lent it a completely different meaning. To the extent that words possessed any permanent sense or meaning, his were a tad hair-raising.

An observer familiar with Doctor Mephisto's methods would no doubt imagine all kinds of things upon hearing him announce that he "must try" to accomplish something. And Yakou? No matter how flexible his imagination, the scene that unfolded next stretched it even further.

"That's a good boy. I'm opening the door."

Mephisto's voice reverberated enchantingly in the blue examination room. A neophyte might have expected the manner of a mother pacifying a child awakened by a bad dream. Or a young man soothing a weeping lover. Or a grandparent humoring a sullen grandchild.

But no. The figure of the Demon Physician addressing the black casket instead resembled Charon, the mysterious and powerful ferryman of Hades who guided the deceased to the land of the dead.

There came a reply.

The casket trembled slightly as the black panels again rearranged themselves. A low moan began to leak out, communicating both bitterness and resentment. The panels encased the sleeping, roasted corpse. The frightened corpse. Frightened by the sweet murmurs of an incubus that would lull the wildest of animals to sleep.

"That's a good boy. There's nothing to be afraid of. Anyone who is ill and wishes relief is my patient."

He touched the lid of the casket and leaned in closer, showing just a glimpse of a countenance filled with infinite compassion.

"I see. It is too bright in here. In that case—"

The room was immediately engulfed in dark blue shadows. The real surprise came next. Calm descended. The thing inside the casket was following the lead of his attending physician. This was Demon City after all.

But the man in the casket was still surely mad.

"Open up, my good patient."

The voice of this artist further colored the already blue world. It seemed impossible, but the casket was yielding its secrets. Yakou saw the eyes of the monster lying there in the darkness light up with hope.

A white finger reached forth from the mists of Hades and touched the ravaged face. Doctor Mephisto said, "Accept me, and I will grant you what you desire."

"Doctor Mephisto. The Demon Physician." Yakou's voice, trembling with admiration, faded off into the distance.

When Takako Kanan came to this city, she'd tried to master the mental self-control techniques taught by the tour guides. She absorbed the *qi* of the earth up through the soles of her feet and stored it in her belly, then released it like a breath through her spine. By teaching herself self-hypnotic techniques, she could keep her wits about her no matter what happened.

She wasn't frightened of what might emerge from the shadow box. After three days in Demon City, she'd gotten used to the weirdness. And Takako had her own smarts on top of that. It wasn't her own thoughts that made her cower and turned the blood in her veins to ice. It was the unearthly *qi* being cast off. The *qi* welled up and came at her like a wind.

The soles of her feet grew warm. The hot currents vanished around her ankles.

"My, my. What interesting skills you have."

The voice behind her contained a curious touch of humanity. "Miss, you seem to be familiar with our circumstances. And your connection with Setsura Aki?"

"Um—" The sound squeezed out of her throat. She was keeping a remarkably good grip on herself. She felt a surge of self-confidence. But the paralysis did not lessen. "I'm the one who brought you here."

"And why would you do such a thing?"

There was a teasing edge to his voice, a blend of sincerity and curiosity. This undoubtedly reflected the presence of a human soul. A sense of calmness grew in Takako's breast. But she held her tongue. She knew that the owner of the voice was something other than human. To admit she'd brought him here so that Setsura could apprehend him would be as good as signing her own death sentence.

"In any case, I thank you for going to the effort. But you must be aware of our true natures?"

Contrary to her own wishes, Takako felt her eyes opening as wide as they could.

"Your silence speaks volumes. Miss, how much do you know?"

His voice was nearer now.

"N-nothing—" Her teeth chattered. "I-I don't know anything."

"Please calm down. I am feeling a bit peckish, but I am not so crass as to assault a young lady to whom I am so indebted. I shall leave it to others to lay claim to that pretty neck of yours." A short pause. "You, there. Enter."

He was addressing somebody other than her. At first, Takako thought it was the shop girl. Then she heard the door leading into the storage alcove creak open.

The light in the storage alcove still wasn't turned on. The alcove was darker than the office, but the faint glow of the summer evening still slanted through the air. The outlines of several human shadows marked the ground there. At a glance, it was obvious from their features and clothes that these were rough men accustomed to violence.

Four of them.

"I have been observing the situation since I was awakened from my nap. What is your purpose for being here? Well, regardless, my agenda is full."

Takako felt a ball of ice form in her stomach. She tried to turn around but couldn't make herself look at him.

The yakuza thugs saw what she could not.

The overhead light in the office was behind him, turning his face into a silhouette. But something glittered in the middle of his forehead. His long, luxurious black hair was braided with gems and shining baubles.

To describe his height as "soaring" would be no exaggeration. The black fabric of his clearly Chinese clothing covering his resplendent frame was woven with golden threads. By the common sense of the outside world, he was entirely out of place.

But there was nothing out of place about him here. Everybody had the right to live—and dress—the way they wanted to in Demon City. Still, what was that thing glittering in the middle of his forehead?

His eyes burned, as if erupting with fiery cravings within. What he wanted right now was *them.*

"W-We were asked—" the one in front stammered. His lips seemed glued together. "—That girl, that box-thing she took, the owner wants it back. He let a valuable thing go for a song. We came to get it."

The shadowed face slowly turned and looked at the storage alcove. The contours of the shadow box were slowly staining the surrounding area like a drop of India ink falling into clear water.

"What it comes down to, buddy, if you want it that bad, it's time to ante up or get out of the game."

The silhouette didn't reply to the challenge. Instead he said, "Woman. Given the situation as described, is it true that you purchased it?"

"Yes," Takako answered honestly. She knew she should have considered the consequences of dealing with that particular curio shop more carefully. But at the time, she'd earnestly suppressed the questioning voice in her head.

"So, how shall we resolve this? Exchange it for the price paid or demand a king's ransom?"

His inquiry was sincere. He spoke as would any businessman honestly concerned with sealing the deal, in everyday language entirely out of place with the present circumstances.

That frightened Takako more than anything. She wanted it to end already. "Do as you please. Just take it and leave."

"That does leave me in something of a fix, it still being light out. Well, fine. As the lady said, take it and leave."

The men hesitated, confused. Once they'd extracted the whereabouts of the item from the cab driver, their job was to extort from the customer several times the agreed-on price. To simply return with it not a penny richer would yield them no more profit than what it'd sold for.

But today's work was already pretty much par for the course. "Got it. Sorry, no refunds. That all goes to our shipping and handling fees."

The silhouetted face smiled broadly. The thugs pretended to ignore him and turned their attention instead to the shadow box, though with the feeling that today was really turning out not to be their day at all.

"Hey." The yakuza who'd been doing all the talking jerked his jaw at the underlings behind him. They surrounded the shadow box and reached out in a collective bear hug.

Three grunts, and then *"Shit!"* filled the storage alcove. When they'd tried to lift it up, three pairs of hands sank *into* it instead. And whatever was inside it sent a sensation racing along their fingers, as if they had plunged their hands into a pool of water.

Not being able to lift it did not mean there was nothing there to *feel*.

"*That* is the product of five hundred shadows—cast by five hundred pregnant women in their ninth months—stitched together. A woman about to give birth is particularly sensitive to human terrors. She will go to any extreme to protect the child in her belly. That is the time when it is easiest to separate body and soul. The body and the shadow that runs after it are the most different. The women who had their shadows stolen all died, of course. Such a cruel thing to do."

At some point, as he descended upon the storage area with leaden steps, a sorrowful note tinged the man's voice. "This box of shadows assimilates itself to darkness. If you still have no objections, then by all means take it with you."

"Give me a fucking break."

The thugs at last returned to thuggish form. Purple veins stood out on their foreheads. A yakuza's most reliable weapon was the sheer unpredictability of his crazy-ass actions once the fighting started.

For Shinjuku, the man in Chinese dress standing in front of them and the shadow box itself were hardly eye-openers. These knuckle-draggers didn't have the slightest idea what a shadow box was or what it could be used for.

"You want a piece of us? Is that it? It's up to you. We'll be taking this girl with us until you figure it out."

"The birth of violence is the death of trust and

honor." Solemn undertones echoed in the dark voice. "The nature of man is evil. But that is why this city is made for us." A voice layered with strata upon strata of impenetrably dense sounds, as if resounding from the deepest ocean depths.

The lead thug swung his right fist, slanting upwards and connecting with the man's solar plexus. Landing unparried, the blow would have ruptured any other man's spleen.

Feeling a strange response in his hand, the yakuza looked down at where his fist had met the man's body. The man hadn't closed his eyes at the moment of impact. His massive palm was wrapped around the thug's fist. The thug hadn't even seen his arm move.

He tried to kick at the man's shins but never finished the motion. His fist tightened as it collapsed under the pressure. The thug threw his head back and screamed. Bones creaked and shattered. Like twigs snapping underfoot. The screams grew louder and longer.

The broken fist twisted unrelentingly clockwise. An audible *crack!* and the thug's wrist rotated a full one hundred eighty degrees. He fainted from the pain. The man thrust him out of the way.

The mouths of the remaining three twitched as if they'd each bit down on a raw lemon. They'd each crushed a capsule hidden in a false molar. The liquid drained directly into the stomach, where it was absorbed into the bloodstream faster than an injection.

The transformations began at once.

Their bodies turned white, white because of the white hairs sprouting all over their bodies. The hair had the toughness and resilience of high-tension wire. It would repel a round from a handgun as easily as it would a blow from a nightstick.

Their muscles expanded and rippled like magma domes swelling out of the ground. The yakuza groaned, this time because of the pleasure of power filling their bodies. Necks and shoulders expanded like inflating inner tubes, fangs and claws exploded outwards, engorged with sinister desires.

The silhouetted face looked dispassionately upon these white apes dressed in human clothes. "What lucky creatures you are. All the more *qi* for me to suck out of you."

The great ape took aim at the man's forehead with four-inch hooked claws that could rip through an elephant's hide.

But first the man touched his right hand to his chest. The first yakuza ape noted that there were only two fingers left on his hand.

A second later, the ape was dead. The body was sent flying out the door, along with the other two still-standing thugs, landing in the tiny garden. They didn't spring immediately to their feet. They groaned, holding back the shadows closing in on them.

When the flying body hit them, they felt a cold wind blow through them, strangely draining their energy. It was like standing over an open grave.

The Chinese man charged through the open door to where the gloom had already transformed into an inky darkness. The yakuza grunted as the fierce *qi* beat against their faces like a flurry of blows from a heavyweight boxer. The giant apes were reduced to a pair of piñatas.

"I've got no use for beasts, even if they're only humans pretending to be beasts. Depart." The rebuke lashed at them like a whirlwind spinning across an empty desert.

The chemically mutated yakuza took off like they'd been bounced off a trampoline, vaulting a low fence and running away. Were it not for the sheer terror seared onto their faces, the sight would have resembled a scene from a circus.

Takako sensed him coming back into the room. She did not turn around. Though the mental shackles binding her had dissolved, she could not summon the courage to face the inhabitant of the shadow box.

She heard a moan from the yakuza collapsed in pain on the floor of the storage area. His condition only added to the swirling dark confusion and cruel foreboding that smothered her like a wet blanket. Another presence invaded that space, and then she heard him being launched through the air.

"Right now I could even indulge in the blood of a brigand."

The meaning of his words didn't register. Takako's mind spun. Then came a long *gaack*. She didn't want to think about what would make a human being imitate a strangled duck.

A thick knot of bile welled up in her throat. She desperately choked it down. A sharp smell arose. Then a splat like that made by a bucket of water thrown against a wall. She didn't think about what caused it.

Ahh—somebody gasped. Then the sound of drinking. Takako felt as if hours were passing. The drinking continued.

How soon until daybreak, she wondered. Wasn't this Demon City? What would be the best way to use a shadow box? Maybe she should take it home. Her father the archeologist would tell her to give it to a museum, or return it to the Chinese government. How to persuade him otherwise?

She noticed that the gasping had diminished. The smell stung at her nose and penetrated the air. With every breath it stained her lungs and gut.

"Woman." He softly called out to her. He was perversely relaxed. "Get out of here."

She didn't know how to respond.

"Hurry. If you do not, I shall no longer contain myself. It was not worth the drinking, of course. I am not satisfied—"

Takako's throat constricted. She tried to speak, but nothing came out. What was this man trying to say? The dawn would soon break.

"What are you doing?" the voice urged. A strange voice, as if irritation and intoxication were battling violently with each other. "Go, now. *No, stay.* But go—"

She knew she must flee. She knew as well that he wasn't stopping her. And she knew that he'd come flying at her as soon as she took a step.

Takako stood there at her wit's end.

"A good thing you didn't go," he said with increasing confidence. "I thank you. If my armies had been made up of women like you, they would never have seen defeat. Come."

Takako shook her head and stared down at her feet. The drab little office covered with tatami mats. The teacup on the table half-filled with now-cold green tea. It didn't look like she was ever going to get that refill.

And then—and then—the air touched her back and neck. He was behind her. "You have a beautiful throat."

At some point, the heavy, male reverberations in

his voice had disappeared. The breath striking her ear lewdly trembled with hunger and desire.

Something wet trailed along the right side of her neck. Takako was seized with unbelievable disgust and joy. This is what *that* felt like. It was exactly as the legends promised. This was why the victim looked forward to each visitation. Why she opened the windows, took the garlands of garlic from around her neck, opened her negligee and exposed her breasts. And waited for the night to deepen.

Hurry—The masochistic impulse throbbed in the veins of her neck. *"Quickly,"* she said aloud.

The pressure of his lips against her neck increased. And then his moist tongue. This was her reward. Having accosted the girl's white neck, his mouth slid along her shoulder. The sensation was like thousands of delicate daddy-longlegs feeling their way along, oozing warm oil from their bodies.

Violate me, she implored. *Poison my body and my soul with your blood.*

His lips returned again to where they'd begun. Takako shook with anticipation, with the all-too-human eagerness to violate human law. His tongue retreated, replaced by something hard and cold.

"Ahh—" A gasp of delight. The fangs sank deeper. Her pleasure and fear surged towards the limits of human toleration. Her vision dimmed.

Just as suddenly the light increased. The fangs withdrew. Her body writhed. At the same time that haunting mouth and fangs released her, her human reason and sense of shame returned.

Still she could not turn around. A ghostly *qi* greater

than before commanded it.

There were two silhouettes behind her now. The black-clad Chinese man turned to the figure in the storage area. In the darkness, the brilliant beauty of his features put even the moon to shame.

"It seems we have a guest," the comely voice said.

The owner of Aki Senbei had returned.

Chapter Two

"Setsura Aki?"

The question was posed with a detached air, the hints of hellish hunger gone. The manner in which it was asked could even suggest an air of propriety and politeness.

"Have you been waiting long?"

At a glance, Setsura had surely summed up the situation and the nature of his "guest." Yet his question was equally calm and mellifluous.

"This is not the first time we have met. I observed you from the deck of the ship. I am Ryuuki."

"The pleasure is all mine."

And he sincerely meant it. He didn't move from the storage area. The bloody body of the yakuza thug lay at his feet.

"Pardon me for asking, but did you happen to visit the ward government building today?"

"And how would you know that?"

"Thanks to you, I had to pay a visit to the hospital. The ward mayor was there. It seems that this city has a new practitioner of the dark arts who can move through the night in the middle of the day. I catch a whiff of it floating around here as well."

"You are as I expected. A pity you should waste those skills as a private detective."

"Well, it is only a side job. But seeing as you are capable of springing unexpectedly from a cover of darkness, what are you doing here? Now?"

Setsura addressed the question as he would to a friend, as if fully expecting an answer.

"I had planned on visiting the Toyama housing project before coming here. But I couldn't quite shake off that bungled effort at the mayor's office. I, who was unable to take on a single decrepit witch by himself, was left behind in this shadow box. The next thing I knew I found myself here. This girl filled me in on the details."

Setsura's eyes communicated his surprise. He hadn't imagined that his opposite would speak in so freely a manner. "Makes sense. The old man was by himself."

"So you have met Sir Kikiou?"

"We had a bit of a dust-up."

"And you came away unharmed."

"Oh, I wouldn't go that far. He gave as good as he got. If I'd been there alone, we might all be arranging my wake this evening instead."

"No mean feat, fighting Sir Kikiou and living to tell the tale. He grossly underestimated you."

Ryuuki bared his gleaming teeth and laughed loudly. The husky laughter swirled around the storage area and the back office like a small gale.

"What a pleasant surprise, seeing him rocked back on his heels like that. He certainly must regret leaving me behind now. Not everything goes the way he expects it to. I hope he enjoyed a taste of his own medicine. I shall be the one to return with your head and his name shall be dust."

Setsura answered the extravagant boast by closing his eyes and nodding. *Sure, I get where you're coming from*, he seemed to be thinking. "So I take it you plan on leaving with my head?"

"That I will," Ryuuki answered brightly, disarmingly so.

"The woman must be out of harm's way first."

"Of course."

Setsura glanced at Takako. "Can you walk?"

"Yes," she said. And then, "No, I can't."

"Well, then—"

Before Setsura had stopped speaking, Takako felt a slight, acupuncture-like prick on the back of her neck. The paralysis left her feet a moment later. The work of Setsura's devil wires.

"Get out of here. Through that door to the shop. I'll bring you up to date later."

"Yes!"

Takako ran toward the door. One step through the door, and her feet took on a life of their own.

The door banged shut, and Setsura said, "Where do you want to do this?"

"Anywhere you want."

"Anywhere I want? There could be traps around here everywhere."

"All the traps in the world won't help you when death taps you on the shoulder. We all go to our doom when our time is up. I've always believed that."

"How sporting. I never would have taken you for one of Kikiou's subordinates."

"I am no one's subordinate."

"I apologize."

"Though I hardly possess a status worthy of such a boast. Running freely across the endless steppes in pursuit of the Hun King—how long ago was that?"

"So you have chased the setting sun?"

The man smiled broadly. "And will this city also set?"

"Yes."

"So you are familiar with that tint and that color?"

"Yes." Setsura's voice brightened as well, as if nothing delighted him more than talking of sunsets.

"I saw it in the western deserts far from the capital. You have seen it too, from the western reaches of this accursed city? You know what it means to chase the setting sun?"

"A long time ago."

"I see." He nodded, like the older brother silently accepting the opinion of the younger.

"And nowadays?"

"My moonlighting keeps me busy. But now and then."

"Humans love the sunrise and loathe the sunset. Especially the citizens of such a prosperous capital. We have seen much in our lives. Both joy and sadness. But more of sadness."

"A tumbleweed or dust in the wind—at times I feel that way. But it comes with the territory."

Those who bent like the grass, floated like the clouds, and calmly went where the breezes took them, to a place where no hearts could be broken—there were times when Setsura wished he could be like them too.

Ryuuki asked, "And what would this moonlighting be?"

"Chasing after the Hun King, earning a little on the side, and trying to balance the books in the meantime."

Ryuuki smiled at the nonsensical answer. "And what do you do?"

"I look for missing persons."

"That is not your main line of work?"

"That would be running this *senbei* shop."

"And looking at sunsets. You are an odd man."

"Thank you."

"What a strange relationship this is. In this place of death I meet a man with whom I wouldn't mind talking the night away."

Setsura shrugged. "That'd be fine with me too."

"I'm sorry, but that is out of the question. Princess is keeping this body alive."

Ryuuki's mouth briefly turned down in an expression of self-derision. He smoothly recovered. His calm and shining eyes began to change in color, began to turn red.

Setsura stood there. At ease. Like dust in the wind, like a blade of grass bending in a breeze, taking a pose that adapted itself to every variable in the environment around him.

Ryuuki's malevolent *qi*.

Setsura's devil wires.

"One thing," Setsura said.

"What?"

"The koto you played at the hospital that put us to sleep. Why didn't you use it tonight?"

"I was in no mood for a fight that night. Now I am facing off against a true warrior. I could never live with the disgrace of taking a head by such means."

A faint smile rose to Setsura's lips.

Then Ryuuki's right forearm separated below the elbow. It took another moment to become clear that it had actually been cut away. Ryuuki heard a faint hum beyond the hearing of a normal human—from his right elbow toward his throat.

The arm tumbled onto the tatami, scattering fresh blood like the end of a spinning hose, sticking the landing with a jerk, its remaining two fingers spread apart and pointing skyward.

The mysterious force stretched between the ceiling and the floor. Ryuuki leapt in a single motion to the back of the room, thrusting his left hand out in front of him. As if with its last gasp, flopping over and growing purple, the right arm directed its *qi* into the strand of Setsura's devil wires, deflecting it and staving off a second attack.

"Like a rolling tumbleweed, eh?"

Taking aim at the upright Setsura, Ryuuki's demon *qi* shot at him. The figure in the black duster staggered and fell to his knees. But he didn't collapse. Perhaps it hadn't contained a sufficient killing force.

Frustration flickered in Ryuuki's eyes as he summoned his energy for another attack. But then Ryuuki froze. In the very moment before impact, the countenance of the beautiful manhunter changed into that of a different person.

"What? Compassion will be the death of you."

On one knee, head bowed, the haunting, mellifluous voice flowed across the room. He was the same Setsura, but not the same at all.

"You severed my *qi*," Ryuuki grumbled under the breath.

His face still hidden from view, the *other* Setsura said, "You've done well enough to send me to the hospital. But your right arm is now useless. Both my hands are fine. Shall we see who is the fastest?"

Ryuuki hesitated. A split second later, the fierce fighting spirit shone in his eyes. He raised his left arm, again clenched his five fingers, and cast his eyes forward.

"I sense one too many obstacles before me now.

Perhaps a return engagement—"

The words hadn't left his mouth before he vaulted through the window of the back office. The glass exploded outwards like a fireworks display and the night swallowed him up.

Startled shouts came from outside, repeated cries of "Freeze!" Gunfire followed.

A brief silence.

Setsura was still down on one knee when a squad of officers decked out in flak jackets and SWAT gear barreled into the room, right arms jabbed out in front of them.

"B-Boss?" cried out the shop girl, behind them. Takako was with her.

The SWAT officers stepped into the storage area and put their arms around Setsura's shoulders to help him up. And then grunted in obvious distress and stepped back.

The officers wore special thermal gloves that insulated against heat, cold and electric current. They were made from fabric proven to resist the harshest Siberian winter. But touching Setsura all but turned their fingers to icicles. They yanked off their gloves to find their fingers turning blue.

"W-What the hell—!"

Mistakenly believing that Setsura was deliberately causing this reaction, their colleagues pivoted and pointed their right arms at him. Each had a 4 mm caliber automatic mounted on his forearm. It was synced to a heads-up display inside his sunglasses that tracked and aimed along his line of sight. Despite the small caliber, the rounds contained high-explosive charges that would make short work of a grizzly bear.

"I meant to tell you not to touch me." Setsura

sounded like an old man on his last legs.

"Are you all right?"

The shop girl pushed through the scrum of SWAT officers and ran up to him. She stepped right on the yakuza's bloody torso but didn't seem to notice. She was a citizen of Demon City, after all. Takako followed after her.

The shop girl said, "What's going on? I didn't have a clue until this girl told me."

"Has the ambulance arrived?" asked the *senbei* shop owner in his normal voice.

If the SWAT teams hadn't arrived when they did, he'd be a dead man. A multipurpose armored personnel carrier that doubled as a critical-car ambulance had been dispatched at the same time.

"Setsura, where are you hurt?" Takako's voice shook. The shop girl stood in her way, not knowing who she was or what was her intent.

"Can you walk?" asked one of the SWAT officers. The man with frostbit fingers had already left to summon the ambulance.

"More or less. What about the target?"

"He ran off," the SWAT officer quickly answered. He had a magnificent moustache and the approximate build of a small boulder. "We gave chase, but he gave us the slip. Still, anybody who'd invade the home of Setsura Aki and wound him before taking off is one bad character."

"There's no point in pursuing him, Kusama-san. Call back your troops. Let's not add to the body count."

"Hey, you remembered my name." Kusama thumbed the mike in his left hand and ordered his men back to base. "It's an honor, sir. I was hoping I could settle my debt to you today, but it looks like that will have to wait."

"You showing up was salvation enough," Setsura said, deadly serious.

"You're in bad shape. The EMTs will be here soon."

"You probably don't have a good way of transporting a patient without touching him. Well, here goes—"

Setsura gathered his remaining strength in his legs. It felt like digging a buried boulder out of the ground. He slowly lifted his head.

The shop girl let out a strangled cry. Takako's eyes went wide.

The wan, sunken cheeks of the beautiful man's face made him look like the walking dead.

Chapter Three

Yakou gazed thoughtfully at the man sitting next to him. Reflected in the window opposite, the faces looked back at him. The two of them. So much beauty multiplied by two seemed only to deepen its incomprehensible depths.

With the long black hair spilling down like an ocean wave, the white cape cloaking his whole body seemed to glow with a light from within. Such was the nature of his striking features.

They were speeding through the Shinjuku night in a limousine. Yakou couldn't shake from his thoughts the incredible sight he'd witnessed in the hospital examination room only thirty minutes before. The object of his admiration had restored the sanity of the mad vampire policeman who'd previously appeared beyond all hope.

It'd only taken him an hour. Even more remarkably, the cure hadn't required any medical instruments. He'd restored the light of reason in the policeman's eyes using only his hands and the soft sound of his voice.

Touching the forehead of the patient, these fingers that Yakou could imagine pressing against the fingerboard of a Stradivarius deftly sank through the flesh.

And when he withdrew them, no mark was left behind on the skin, not one drop of blood left on the fingers. This doctor who lived outside the world of normal human morality then whispered enticingly into the ear of the prone policeman, in a manner utterly appropriate to the name *Mephisto*.

The old philosopher kings would have happily sold their souls to hear the words he spoke.

At length, the white-clad doctor turned to his companion and said, "The treatment is complete. Proceed with sire expropriation."

"Understood."

Like a student taking direction from the professor, Yakou nodded. He tilted his head slightly back. When he straightened again, a white pair of fangs jutted modestly from the corners of his mouth.

Without any dramatic gestures, the young man approached the gurney and leaned over the exposed throat. Several seconds later, he lifted his head.

"You may wake him up," he said to Mephisto, hiding his mouth behind his hand.

"He is awake."

Yakou turned around. The police officer was sitting up, his eyes vacant. So vacant that he could believe that if poked in the eye, the finger would sink to the back of the eye socket. Empty caverns whistling with a cold wind.

"How are you feeling?" Mephisto asked the haggard-looking Yakou.

"Not well. But I'll manage. This man's sire is a species apart. It took a lot out of *me* as well."

His use of the personal pronoun *boku* prompted a double-take from Mephisto. "Do you usually refer to yourself as *boku*?"

"On more formal occasions."

"And other than that?"

"I tend to use *ore*," he said, citing the "tougher," more "masculine" first person pronoun.

"Weren't you raised in London?"

"Yes, but I get the feeling people don't take *boku* seriously. Not for somebody my actual age."

"Then you should stick to *ore*. It's always better for people to be at home in their own skins."

"Understood," said Yakou without reservation.

Mephisto pointed at the police officer. "Let's begin the questioning."

Yakou nodded. "Who is your sire?"

A long silence. Then the cop's voice tore at the quiet, as if born from a netherworld where the damned writhed in the fires of hell. *"Y-You—are—"*

Two pairs of crimson lines trickled from both sides of his neck. When the vampire's prey transformed into the blood-craving beast, the abominable scars in his neck disappeared. They had appeared again, contending with the new wounds and with the new sire.

During sire expropriation—when another vampire took the blood of a victim already transformed—the manifestation of an anemic state in the prey was not by itself enough to cement a new master/servant relationship.

Rather, the new vampire wishing to expropriate the old sire could only do so if his power and authority could compete with that of the first vampire.

In any case, a showdown between the two forces was unavoidable. The struggle within the victim could be just as damaging to the body and mind of his new sire. Consequently, sire expropriation posed a grave risk even to vampires with eternal lives.

Nevertheless, by taking the blood of a vampire's victim, otherwise unknowable details about the sire's character and circumstances would come to light. That was why Yakou, and before him the Elder, were willing to undergo the ordeal. It was not clear how deeply implanted this instinctual loyalty was, but it prevented knowledge from being lightly revealed to another person.

Only a powerful new sire could demand a similar degree of fealty and uncover that information.

As if arriving at a sufficiently satisfactory breakthrough, Yakou clung to the railing of the gurney, steadied his breath, and cleared his throat.

"Where is the abode of your former sire located?"

And that was how they had come to be in the limousine, racing through the Demon City night.

Under "normal" circumstances, they would have waited until morning. But because of the internal struggle aroused at the moment of "sire expropriation," the vampire who'd originally taken the police officer's blood might sense his own defeat and go on the lam. Hence the decision to strike at once.

There should be nothing in the Shinjuku darkness that could equal the combined forces of the Elder's grandson and Doctor Mephisto.

Mephisto turned to him. Yakou averted his eyes. More than his beauty, the Doctor's gaze left him feeling unsettled and abashed, an emotion he had difficulty explaining to himself. The Doctor didn't seem to notice, and Yakou presently returned the look. Then—

"Stop the car."

Before the command died away, the car lurched forward and back. Mephisto opened the door himself and stepped into the black world.

His white cape fluttered like a delicate flower in the breeze, like the ghostly moonflower that bloomed only at night. The wind played plaintively at his black hair. The mountains of rubble lining the shoulders of the road were a vast, white wasteland beneath the street lights.

Yakou ran over to him. They had detected something from the inside of a car going sixty miles per hour. The two of them stared into the blackness.

"You see it?" Mephisto eventually asked, apparently giving up on getting a closer look.

"Yes. A white shadow skipping along the rubble."

"A woman."

"I couldn't tell. Was it?"

"Do you feel the cold?"

"Now that you mention it." Yakou's eyes gleamed. "And undoubtedly because of *her*."

"I would dearly like to believe otherwise, but that does seem to be the case. However—"

"However?"

Under Yakou's doubtful gaze, Mephisto said reluctantly, "A beautiful woman."

This young man had still not plumbed all the depths of this doctor's disposition. "You don't say," he replied shortly. He casually made note of the obvious. "One of *them*."

"Probably. This is their time."

"So there'd be no point in continuing the pursuit at this juncture."

"We need to know where she is going. That should soon become clear. One way or another."

Yakou was at a loss for words.

"Let us believe that the Elder and Setsura Aki have got our backs. Think of the night as their friend and our enemy."

"I understand."

"We should be on our way."

Mephisto turned and closed his eyes. In his mind's

eye he saw the woman atop the mountains of wreckage running off into the distance. Her white dress was like a flower left behind by a fleeing lover. More than her unmarred expression of joy as she danced through the night, it was her unequaled beauty that put his own to shame.

He was not unconscious of the fact.

The car stopped ten minutes later. The rolling hills of rubble looked even more insurmountable than before. Shinanomachi Station, the place Officer Hyuuga had revealed to them. They were in front of the gates to the former Keio University Hospital campus.

The driver reported, “The infrared scanners show no signs of human activity within a half-mile radius.”

“*Human* activity, eh?” Mephisto muttered. “Let's go.”

The limo silently bore these two soldiers in an army of darkness into the great expanse of the debris field. A midnight battle was about to begin.

Part 7:
The Sirens Of Shinano

Chapter One

The wind came from far away. Less a wind than a current in the air. Stronger gusts opposing it immediately retreated. If the breezes shifted around and blew just as fiercely from the same quarter, they wouldn't be the same as the first.

This fleeting, ephemeral thing would be found nowhere else.

The wind whipped unimpeded across the great expanse of land surrounding the enormous buildings. It sailed on alone, whistled through an overgrown stand of pine trees, leapt a rusted bicycle, a corroding park sign, a street light that was falling apart while it continued to shine. It swirled around a concrete wall and past steel shutters rusted shut.

It danced past an armored SUV equipped with a 20 mm machine cannon and a flame thrower. Past the guards armed with shotguns, and Magnum pistols strapped to their hips. Over the children playing in the courtyard and the couples strolling down the sidewalks that crisscrossed the park. Deeper inside the grounds.

With its final breath, the gust of wind mounted the hill and spotted its objective. It drew closer and caressed the nape of his neck.

The Elder stood with his hands locked across the small of his back. He released his hold and touched the back of his neck with one hand. Perhaps an insect had paused in flight there. He scratched the skin with the nail of his index finger.

From the crest of the hill he looked down on the world below. The windows of the apartment buildings glowed with light. The streetlamps wound around the buildings like strings of glowing pearls.

He heard the sound of a guitar and people singing. "The Windmills of Your Mind." The youngsters in the park preferred American classics to those of their own country. This always gave the old-timers something to gripe about. But such was life.

He was standing atop "Mt. Hakone," a tad east of the center of the Toyama municipal housing project. The highest elevation in Shinjuku.

It was more a modest hill than a mountain. During the height of summer, the fragrance of the mountain lilies grew suffocating. The pretty buds of the evening primrose swayed next to clumps of oleander. A wonderful place to take a stroll.

With its view of the gleaming outlines of the "Sunshine Building" to the north in neighboring Ikebukuro, and the skyscraper district to the southwest in the new heart of the city, the narrow platform at the top of this "mountain" did instill a sense of standing at the commanding heights.

The Elder's long sigh was carried away by the wind. It was his job to protect all those peaceful lives going on beneath him.

"I first heard your name when I was a child." The gnarled old voice carried far. "What do your four thousand years of wisdom have to offer me?"

"All you will know is the meaning of death." There was a touch of smugness in her answer. And a kind of elegance. The white shadow stood behind the Elder.

"The last thing the living ever learn is that nothing lasts forever."

"Then I must thank you." The Elder slowly turned around. "Death—the true end of life—is a wonderful thing."

The white shadow smiled, as if to empathize.

"How should I address you?" the Elder asked politely.

He wasn't being forward. It was an earnest expression of respect for this lovely woman who had lived at least another lifetime longer than him.

"My name is whatever you wish it to be."

"Then, according to the old legends, I call you Princess."

"That is a good name."

Stirred by the wind, her hair stroked her alabaster features. She wore no decorations in her hair. Her luxuriant black tresses hung freely down to her waist.

"For what purpose have you come here?"

"I do not know."

"You don't know?"

"Do you think some *purpose* guided me through the last four thousand years? But if compelled to articulate one—there is life in this city. And vice. Swirling whirlpools of hatreds and curses. That is all that comes to mind. Though I venture Kikiou would say differently."

"I know. Based on his actions thus far, his purpose is the subjugation of this city. Except that the best-laid plans are made to be broken. I wonder why that is?"

"Are you referring to what happened in Chang'an? Or to those two cities adjacent to the Dead Sea? Kikiou's desires do not always agree with mine. I wish to live free. Sleep when I wish. Drink when I wish. Sing when I wish. Apparently that is not enough to satisfy him."

"Can't you live here forever in peace?" the Elder asked, the same way a loving mother might speak to her dear, sickly child. "There are two hundred of our compatriots here."

"Live here as *I* wish, I should have said," Princess scoffed. "To drink from whoever *I* want, whenever *I* want, without giving the likes of *you* a second thought."

The Elder's shoulders slumped. But his narrow eyes gleamed with a fierce light. "Why have you visited us this evening?"

"Our original intent was to see you this afternoon with Kikiou and another of my retainers. But an obstacle reared its head right at the beginning. Kikiou suffered a setback and the other is presently incommunicado. There are frightening things afoot in this city. So I have come here. Think of me as the ambassador of Kikiou's intentions."

"Remarkable. And I thought the two of you did not see eye to eye."

"I told him to suit himself."

Princess grinned. The tips of her fangs peeked out from the corners of her rosy red lips. Even they were strikingly attractive. To look at her hands was to desire being struck by them. To look at her feet was to desire being trampled by them. And her white teeth—to desire them to plunge deeply into the heart. Such were the arousing charms of her strangely bewitching beauty.

"There's one more thing I wish to ask you," the Elder said. "What do you intend to do after sending this senior citizen to his grave?"

"I don't really know. But Kikiou intends to exterminate all of your kind."

"I have no intention of offering up my life to you."

"Oh, I have heard that said so many times before."

Princess quickly closed the distance between them. The platform atop Mt. Hakone was only ten feet square. She could reach out and touch the Elder. She looked at him and he looked back. As if the living dead should wear burial shrouds even while on the field of battle, she was dressed in a white *cheongsam* and he in a white suit.

The skin of both of them glowed the color of blood.

"Impressive." Princess blinked once. "But fall into the spell of my eyes and you would die in ecstasy. A pity otherwise."

"The one hundred thousand souls of Hsia on one hand, the one hundred twenty thousand of Yin on the other. And here I stand protecting my two hundred. I'm not dead yet."

"It is always our fate to die and leave behind an empty grave."

"True without a doubt," the Elder heartily agreed, stepping forward, his right hand thrusting outwards in a *nukite* karate strike, with only the thumb bent inward.

An onlooker would have observed no tension in the blow. What kind of sorcery was contained within it became evident as his hand touched the supple rise of her breast and immediately sank all the way down to the wrist.

Princess closed her eyes. A sublime expression tinged with pain, that might even resemble prayer.

The Elder felt her whole weight down the length of his arm. "I don't imagine you are pleased that the end of four thousand years should come in a place like this. But rest well. I am sure to join you at some future date."

He withdrew his hand. Not a single drop of blood fell.

Not a single slit or tear marred the fabric of her clothing. The white figure collapsed like a falling flower.

"Your funeral services should be held in accordance with the land of your birth. But I have no idea what age and what era you were born in." He spoke in a tired voice, almost as if expecting a reply.

"Neither do I."

The Elder's eyes flew open. The white face was staring up at him. A red light shone in her eyes.

"Don't move," she softly commanded. "Just stand there." She effortlessly rose to her feet. An intoxicating scent filled the air. "I do not bleed because of any skill of yours. Killing a woman who has lived for four thousand years could never be so simple as that. I expected more from you. Come."

She gracefully raised her right hand, and beckoned in such a manner that the molecules of air must have been aroused by her caressing touch. Like a marionette dangling from the beguiling and beautiful threads, the white-suited man aimlessly stepped toward her.

A white hand clasped him by the shoulders. Princess sweetly smiled. A second later, the smile froze on her face. The Elder's eyes also cast off a blood-red light.

"As I expected. The man Kikiou should have dispatched first possesses the same eyes as mine. Except that I will not let you go."

With that, she easily hoisted him above her head. Struggle as he might, she held onto his shoulder with a hand as strong as iron.

"Crush your head and you would resurrect yourself regardless. But what about this—?"

The grisly sound of tearing flesh and bone drowned out her words as she yanked the Elder's left arm out of its socket. A fountain of blood splashed onto her feet, staining her shoes and the hem of her white *cheongsam.* She flung the arm away, not wanting to be hindered by the bloody thing.

She reached out again with her lissome left arm. Towards his chest. Like he had only moments before, she buried her hand in his body, down to the wrist, tearing through the muscle, wrenching apart the tendons.

The Elder watched silently. The light in his eyes only began to waver as her fingers clamped around his heart.

"Even you will have a difficult time of it with your heart ripped out of your chest. When dispatching our kind, this method is as good as a stake."

Probably because of the spouting blood, the Elder's features were quickly turning a pale shade of green. Princess stared at him long and hard. She trembled with joy. As the word "heart" left her mouth, she withdrew her hand with a single, uninterrupted motion.

Though the gesture was the same as the Elder's, her right hand was cruelly coated in red like a long scarlet glove, the still-beating heart clutched in her fingers.

She released her hold on his body. The Elder tumbled hollowly to the concrete pad. His heart—that timekeeper of life—was already stilled. But still his voice could be heard.

"Splendidly done. But you will regret coming to this city."

Princess's eyes blazed again. When she leaned over the Elder, something wrapped tightly around her hand—the aorta, pulmonary veins, and carotid artery of the heart she had ripped out of his chest.

"Bastard!" she cursed, raising her right fist.

Just then the blood vessels released a gush of

fresh, red blood. The aorta spouted like a fire hose. This was not ordinary blood. A scream—a sound unlike any heard before by mortal ears—burst from her mouth. She jerked back her beautiful head. But purple smoke was already erupting from her skin.

Seeing through her designs, the Elder had stored up this demon blood in his heart. That was what had drained the color from his features.

"That pretty face of yours will never heal," he said with his final breath, words suffused with a great sense of satisfaction. "According to my inquiries, your pride will not allow you to openly parade through this city. And so I do not die in vain. The rest I leave to my grandson—and to—his two—colleagues—"

The Elder's voice trailed off. It did not resume.

"My face—my face—" she moaned in sorrow and horror. She heard voices and racing footsteps approaching behind her.

"Elder-sama!"

"W-Who the hell are you?"

"What's with her face? That heart she's holding—what did you do to him? *Bitch*!"

The men shouting at her were dressed in ordinary street clothes. They weren't the guards who patrolled during the day. During the night, *they* weren't needed. Because *these* men were here.

Their eyes glowed. Fangs sprang into their open mouths. She was only one woman, but they did not attack her all at once. Because there was no way that one woman could have done that to the Elder. The gruesome nature of the death overwhelmed them, like there was a wall around her.

Princess pressed her hand against her face. "Leave me," she said, turning her back to them. "You all were

going to be next. But there are more pressing things I must tend to now. I'll just have to ask you to wait patiently until I return."

"Say what? Murdering scum!"

"The Elder hasn't been his usual self of late. It must have been this whore's fault all along!"

There were four of them. They'd likely been patrolling the foot of Mt. Hakone and had felt the touch of a strange and cold breeze that didn't belong. Further infuriated by the woman turning her back to them, one of them reached forward and grabbed her shining black hair.

She shook her head. The tresses of her hair sliced through his fingers, dropping them to the ground like stubby white worms.

"Shit!" the men shouted, more in shock than fear.

Strands of her hair whipped at their wide eyes, letting loose a spray of blood. Blinded, they groped aimlessly with their hands. With a soft series of *thuds*, Princess's hands flicked as quickly as snapping whips, sending the blood and flesh flying.

The white tornado whirled through the men, cutting them down like stalks of grain before the scythe. It descended straight down the "mountain," decapitating the stands of crocus and turning the lilies into chaff. Residents who'd also detected a strange thing in the air and came running were cut down by the swirling gale. Screams gushed from windpipes along with geysers of blood.

Pandemonium engulfed the grounds.

The taxi racing along Meiji Dori saw a raised hand at the side of the road and screeched to a halt.

"Need a ride?" the driver called out.

The back door popped open. He wasn't concerned about who the passenger might turn out to be. A heavy sheet of airtight, bulletproof glass separated the driver from the back seat. The man who'd invented it and had equipped the two thousand taxis operating in Shinjuku was a hero to the drivers. It'd made the inventor an overnight millionaire to boot.

But as soon as he recognized the figure with heavy-lidded eyes and dressed in torn clothing as a woman, the driver felt an indescribable chill on the back of his neck, and began to question his instinctual decision to nab one last fare.

Before he could shut the door, the woman was in the cab. The numerous dark stains on her white *cheongsam* only heightened his anxieties.

"Where to, ma'am?"

The cheer in his voice was the result of working this street for over twenty years now.

"My head hurts."

She had a light foreign accent and a voice as sweet as honey. The driver was instantly enraptured.

"You sick?"

"I was burned."

"That's terrible."

But hardly unusual in this city. Unless the cops were standing right there with their guns drawn, a Shinjuku taxi couldn't deny a ride even to a wanted serial killer. This driver had once picked up a cyborg cradling its own head in its arms and hauled it off to a repair shop.

"Is it bad? Want me to take a look?"

"That's all right."

"I understand. Mephisto Hospital is your best bet."

She didn't reply.

"He could probably fix you up while you're sitting in the waiting room. He's the Demon Physician, after all."

"Take me there, please."

The woman's voice until now had struck him as high-handed and aloof. Now the taxi driver zealously and happily complied. Not to mention that the side of her face he could see was so damned attractive.

"Hold on tight! Be there in a flash!"

He pressed the accelerator to the floor. Despite its humble fuel source, the liquid propane engine had remarkable acceleration.

Chapter Two

In his study, Naokichi Kumagaki scanned his thick volume of *A History of Crime in Western Europe.* Hearing his wife announce the arrival of a guest, his face clouded over. Even though his home in Yochou was in an established "safety zone," a guest calling after nine o'clock was always cause for alarm.

He'd heard about the attack on the mayor's office that afternoon, and had received a personal communiqué from the mayor himself. Elite bodyguards were posted at the residences of all the movers and shakers in Shinjuku.

Naokichi Kumagaki was the Shinjuku Chief of Police.

When he asked, his wife said it was Hiromi Oribe, the mayor's private secretary. The Chief briefly wondered why the mayor's missing secretary would show up here, but decided to see her and find out.

Following the mayor's orders, four tough-looking guards had been posted at his home as well. All came from a private security company. Kumagaki didn't trust his own subordinates.

His cell phone doubled as an intercom, and he again considered calling the mayor, but didn't. Four or five days before, they'd practically come to blows over increasing the patrols. He had nothing against the man personally, but on that subject, it was like talking to a brick wall.

And he was still in the dark about the vampire

connection to the aforementioned incident.

Hiromi Oribe walked into the living room and quietly sat down on the sofa next to the window. Other than looking a bit pale, nothing about her seemed out of the ordinary.

"Sorry to keep you waiting. I heard you were kidnapped. It's a relief to see you've made it here in one piece."

He spoke with an authoritative masculinity. Hiromi smiled her always charming, feminine smile. She explained that she'd found herself wrapped in an impenetrable darkness and lost track of space and time. When she came to, she was in an alley just up the street.

Fortunately, she remembered the Kumagaki residence from the last time she'd been there with the mayor. So after contacting the mayor's office, she'd headed straight here, the closest safe place she could think of.

She had no idea what had gone on during those missing hours, and her concern for the mayor's welfare after she'd disappeared led Kumagaki to believe he could trust her.

"In any case, you need to rest. I'll get you a sedative. Later we'll go to see the mayor. Tomorrow I'd like you to come down to police headquarters."

"That'd be fine."

"If you'd just hold on for a while. I'll have somebody come from headquarters."

Kumagaki got up and went over to the videophone on one side of the living room. He had picked up the receiver and was dialing the number when a cold breath tickled the back of his neck.

"What—?"

As he turned his head, he felt a strong pressure against his thigh. The secretary's voluptuous, provocative face filled his field of vision. She brazenly slipped her hand inside his robe and down the front of his pajama bottoms, and grabbed hold of his manhood.

That was enough for the Chief to lose a grip on his higher reasoning abilities. The waves of red-hot desire broadcasted themselves at her through his cock. Her hands—as pliant as streams of water—invaded his pajama bottoms and drew him out and stroked him.

"How's that, Chief?"

The purr in her voice and the lust on her face—so unlike the normally crisp and cool public servant—made her seem like a completely different person. He moaned.

Four guards were camped out in the room adjacent to the bright living room, not to mention the other members of his family.

"I see you watching me all the time, asking yourself, *What's beneath that haughty exterior? What are those breasts like? That ass, those thighs.* Go ahead. Tell me I'm wrong."

"I-It's the truth."

"Right now you're picturing the shape of my bra, the cut and color of my panties. How tight they're cupping my breasts and squeezing my butt. Whether the fabric is sheer enough to see my nipples and my crotch? That's right, isn't it?"

She repeated the carnal questions, her insistent fingers stroking the middle-aged man's invigorated erection. "It's all right by me. I'll show you everything you've ever dreamed of. Get on the intercom and tell them not to disturb you for a while."

This heroic public servant, this man entrusted

with the safety of the most dangerous and tumultuous city in the world, surrendered to a hand job. He did as he was told and hung up the phone.

"Stop dawdling," he growled, an animal shaking in anticipation of further sexual treats.

In the living room—where anybody could walk in on them at any time—the mayor's secretary took off her silk blouse. And then her skirt. All that tempting white skin robbed the Chief of his voice.

Though maintaining at all times the facade of a frostily intellectual college coed, reduced to only a white bra and panties, she had a *fuck me* look about her that stood more than a man's hair on end.

"You'll have to do the rest by yourself."

"Ahh—" His eyes bugged out. Saliva foamed at the corners of his mouth. His rough hands seized her around the waist. The bra fell away. It really was a size too small. Her large breasts had been straining to be set free. The indentations from the underwires showed on her skin.

The Chief bent her back and applied his lips to her left breast and nipple. He didn't mind the coolness of the flesh filling his mouth. While he suckled, he slipped his hand inside her panties and massaged the soft mound between her legs. How he'd wanted to fondle that softness. How he'd wanted to eat her up.

Her left breast shining and wet, he set to ravaging her right. Then he fell to his knees and slowly pulled down her panties. The abundant curve of her ass, the bold line of her thighs—all drew to a focus in her black, luxuriant bush.

The panties fell to her ankles. She stepped out of them.

The Chief kissed the inside of her right thigh,

applied the surface of his damp tongue to her skin, like a cat grooming itself. When he reached her rich thicket, Hiromi Oribe uttered a low moan.

Her strong fragrance stained his hands as he searched out her hidden entranceway and plunged in with his tongue. A rumbling purr spilled from her mouth, like that of a large, menacing cat.

After listening to him lap at her for what seemed like hours, she stepped back. "Stand up," she ordered him. He complied. She pulled back the collar of his dressing gown and hung her arms around his neck. "And now for the one true pleasure—"

Her red lips attached themselves to his stout neck, and sucked his blood like a leech.

Ten minutes later, Kumagaki's wife watched nervously as her husband and the mayor's secretary got into his car and raced off on "urgent business." She'd only asked that the secretary be entrusted to the four bodyguards instead. She wasn't comfortable with the way he instructed her not to speak of the mayor's secretary to anybody else.

But she knew from personal experience that the Chief was a man not above resorting to bouts of rage and even physical violence when he didn't get his way. And so she did as she was told.

Chapter Three

A human form emerged in the headlights. A man. He looked like a bum or vagrant. He buried his face in his arms and dove behind an outcropping of rocky debris.

"Doctor—" Yakou called out.

Mephisto was a step ahead of him.

"Stop the car," he ordered.

They were in the middle of the Keio Hospital grounds. At this time of night, it was unlikely that any slumbering *thing* was actually human. It'd be much safer to assume that any "human" was only a creature pretending to be human.

As soon as the car door opened, Mephisto sprinted off in the direction of the mountain of rocks the "man" had disappeared behind.

Beneath the light of the almost-full moon, the ruins took on a cold glow, still as a graveyard. But with the appearance of a single man and the sweep of his pure white cape, the mood of the desolate scene suddenly shifted.

The inorganic rocky mountain seemed to absorb the moonlight. The distant whistle of the wind as well ceased to blow, and instead played a paean to his beauty. Entranced and yet grieving that it could not mingle its atoms with his, the wind sang to Doctor Mephisto.

There was beauty even in his shadow as he circled the mountain.

Yakou raced up behind him. Another mountain sat

in front of them. The path forked in two directions.

"What do you think?" Mephisto asked.

Yakou closed his eyes and then opened them. "I cannot say." There was a barb in his words. "I would think these grounds would be more familiar to you than to me."

"This doctor knows only the grounds of the human body."

"Sorry."

"Something on your mind?"

"No, nothing."

"We needn't concern ourselves with him."

"Understood."

"Stay on your toes."

Yakou didn't answer at first. He didn't know how well Mephisto could see in the dark, but the young vampire's cheeks burned a rosy pink.

"I'll go right. You take the left, Doctor."

"Got it."

The moonlight scattered around them like silver dust as the two parted ways.

It was a strange path. Despite there being no logic to the piles of debris, in the depths of the darkness, the mountains of rubble completely blocked out the buildings further on. Or perhaps this was because they'd been dumped there without any other purpose in mind.

In any case, the winding paths twisted and turned and combined together again, taking one detour after the other, until all sense of direction was lost.

After walking for five minutes, Mephisto stopped in his tracks. "This feels like the meandering back alleyways of Kabuki-cho. But it looks like the end is in sight."

The meaning of the "end" soon became apparent. A dozen or so feet in front of him stood a girl. The word "girl," though, would only describe her face. The fragrance entwined about her sumptuous body radiated with all the ripeness and vigor of a woman in the prime of her youth.

She was wearing a dark green tunic and Chinese trousers. Her black hair was drawn up into buns behind each ear. Setsura would have recognized her on the spot. She was the enchantress Shuuran, one of the gang of four.

She stared back at Mephisto with a dumbfounded look on her face. Perhaps not even an enchantress was immune to the Demon Physician's physical beauty.

"I don't believe it's been our pleasure to meet," Doctor Mephisto said in Chinese. He bowed. "My dialect is Song Dynasty. I hope you understand me."

"You speak well," she said with a dainty toss of her head. "A pretty man in white. Would you introduce yourself? I am Shuuran."

"I am Doctor Mephisto."

"How about that!" She did a good job of containing her uncontained surprise. The tension created by her raw physicality shattered. The moonlight congealed into a raw bloodlust.

"But of course. That strange feeling in the air. You must have brought the copper around and milked the information out of him. A good thing I came back to make sure that vagrant was good and dead. It's up to Princess and me to clean up after Sir Kikiou's messes."

"I see. So, the other one is here as well?"

"No, not here."

"Then where?" Mephisto asked softly. No matter how strange a being he was confronted with, he always proceeded as calmly as if he was filling out a medical chart. The creature did not exist that could throw him off his stride.

Until now—

"She's gone to see the Elder of the Toyama housing project. I'm sure she'll stop by later for tea with you and Setsura Aki."

At the sound of those names, for the first time, a mixture of emotions colored the Doctor's eyes like a light mist. It too soon vanished. He said, "It was I who discerned your whereabouts first. Remind me to give that useless P.I. a piece of my mind."

"If you are referring to *our* kingdom, it is far too early for you to declare victory." Shuuran's eyes glowed red. "I will inscribe the epitaph on your tombstone before you set one foot *there*."

"Alas, I have already entrusted that task to someone else," said Mephisto, a faraway look in his eyes. "It seems you are in need of medical attention as well. To cure you of your overconfidence, among other things."

He spoke almost chattily, as if the reality of the situation was the furthest thing from his mind. But there were graver echoes in his voice as well, pointed enough to make Shuuran blanch. Her quip about the gravestone had rubbed him quite the wrong way.

She reached into the buns of hair behind each ear, plucking out a pair of silver, crescent-shaped ornaments. As he stood there, two streaks of light appeared to pierce Mephisto's neck, traveling another half-dozen yards past him before turning like boomerangs and returning to her hands without diminishing in speed.

Shuuran said, "My combs."

They definitely looked like ordinary silver combs. But the teeth were as sharp as fangs of cold steel, the curved handles like sharpened scythes.

"I'm impressed," Mephisto said softly. "But digging my grave with an ordinary shovel would be easier."

For a brief moment, Shuuran gaped at him, at his untouched neck. "True, if that had been enough to kill you, I would have branded Sir Kikiou a coward forever after. The real fight begins now."

Shuuran raised the comb in her right hand and drew it across her left wrist. The fresh blood spouted like a fountain, beautiful in the moonlight, and splashed onto the ground.

She licked her wrist. The blood stopped flowing. She cast her eyes down at the pool of blood at her feet, then spun around and dashed off into the darkness.

What happened next would have startled anybody but Mephisto. He started after her, but stopped. A strange sound struck his ears. An exquisitely sweet melody. Mephisto's ears alone would have detected that it came from those two silver combs meshing together. The song seemed composed to inspire the listener to chase after the moon and waste his life away listening to lonesome dirges.

The pool of blood rapidly mutated. Something squirmed in the middle of the thick, congealing mass. Earth. But not the natural surface of the ground. Here and there, black dirt could be seen through cracks and fissures. Beneath the blood was asphalt, but it looked to Mephisto's eyes like earth.

A moment later, the squirming was swallowed up by the blood. It stilled, and then in a flash rose up from the center of the black-red tide. It started out as a doll four inches high and quickly grew to eighteen inches.

Eyes emerged, then a nose. The disturbed ground even fashioned itself into clothing.

Another moment later, this doll born from the pool of blood reached the same height as Shuuran. The doll's red lips parted, revealing her white teeth.

"Hey, big guy. Do me."

Mephisto stood rooted to the spot, as if mesmerized by the sound of her voice. Any man hearing those words would fall into the same trance. So he did as he was told and reached out his arms. Such was the magical allure of her words.

Then she was there in front of him. And then climbing up his back. How she moved was impossible to tell.

Mephisto didn't budge.

The doll opened her mouth. A pair of fangs sprang out. She pulled at the collar of his white cape with her little hands and lowered her mouth to the almost-feminine, almost-transparent skin at the nape of his neck.

Uttering sweet, beguiling instructions and stealing away the will of her prey, she attached herself to his neck with movements too quick for the eye to follow. That by itself was fearsome enough magic. Except that the doll's mouth paused.

Her coquettish face trembled. She blinked.

"Go ahead and drink your fill," Mephisto said. "But can you find a well that isn't dry?"

The doll listened for the rush of blood through the blood vessels in order to determine where to sink her fangs. And though she craned her ears and focused her gaze, she couldn't detect the pulse of blood beneath the translucent skin.

Did blood even flow through the veins of the good

doctor? The reason for its existence negated, the doll peeled off his back, dropped to the asphalt and broke into pieces.

"Is that all?" Mephisto asked the darkness. "Then you'll have to answer to me."

He took off after the girl and disappeared into the gloom. He raked his hands through the empty air. It was pitch black. He could see nothing, hear nothing. The sound of the wind and the light of the moon had vanished.

Mephisto pressed forward regardless. It was not clear why he decided to. Nobody could claim to understand how the Demon Physician's mind worked.

A brilliant light abruptly appeared, and his shadow grew long behind him. Other than narrowing his eyes and glancing up at the shining sky overhead, he barely reacted to this unearthly change. The forest rose up around him in a riot of green. Mephisto stood on a narrow path weaving among the trees.

"She left the door open," he said to himself. He started down the walk, not even bothering to glance back over his shoulder.

The path meandered along for another fifty yards. Mephisto stopped. In the middle of the path was a tea table. Sitting on the table, on a golden stand, was an oblong lump of purple amethyst. It was aligned parallel to the ground, the tapered end pointing in his direction.

"Welcome."

A naked woman stepped between Mephisto and the curious piece of amethyst. It wasn't Shuuran. She wasn't nearly as pretty. Her "beauty" more resembled the carnality of an erotic dancer.

Probably less "resembled" than "was." Her hips swayed, exposing her breasts and the inverted triangle between her legs. "Come on in," she said, pointing down with her left hand and reaching out with her right. Her breasts swayed, but with a lively, youthful firmness.

Mephisto approached silently.

"My job is to entertain any visitors who come down this path. You must be the first in a good hundred years."

Her breath smelled like sour fruit. She draped her arms around his neck. The world shimmered in a white light. In the midst of it, Mephisto caught sight of a thin, incandescent line streaking through the air, angled down toward the earth.

The purple light stabbed through the woman's abdomen and reflected off Mephisto's cape. The temperature over the microsecond duration of the pulse peaked at three hundred thousand degrees.

By focusing the sunlight on a crystal to generate a mixed-phase beam of energy, those ancient Chinese alchemists had chanced upon the same principles and materials as the modern ruby laser.

And the woman? An aiming device. The sun above was probably artificial, yet fixed in position. While the crystal could absorb that light energy, there was no guarantee that the enemy would walk right in front of it. With her body and charms, the woman's purpose was to lure the target into the path of the beam.

Her back and stomach belched blue fire where the beam penetrated her body. The skin turned to charcoal. There'd be another woman along to replace her soon enough.

The smell of burning wood drew Mephisto's attention off to the left. The fat trunk of a nearby beech tree was burning just like the woman's torso. The result of the beam that had reflected off his cape. In Demon

City, everybody knew that optical weapons were useless against Doctor Mephisto.

"What a curious device," he said, looking down at the woman's body, which was melting like wax. It could just as well have been a wax sculpture brought to life.

Mephisto walked around the tea table and continued on his way.

She showed up in the after-hours clinic of Mephisto Hospital just past ten o'clock that night. She had a handkerchief pressed against one side of her face. Though struck by the loveliness of the exposed half, the receiving nurse nevertheless was compelled to answer her questions with a cold objectivity.

"The hospital director is currently out. But there are several qualified doctors on call who can treat burns."

The young woman in the white *cheongsam* didn't reply to this customary brusqueness and turned away. At that moment a SWAT officer hurried by her and asked, "What room is Setsura Aki in?"

After scanning and confirming the validity of his ID card, the receiving nurse consulted her computer. She shook her head. "He is not to be disturbed, and he's not allowed to have visitors. He's in the special isolation ward on the seventh floor. No one may see him."

"Listen, young lady—"

"No one's even allowed a glimpse. There's no telling what illnesses a patient confined to the isolation ward in this hospital could have."

"Do you know why I want to see him?"

"It's written all over your face." The nurse lowered her voice. "Are you one of Aki-san's friends?"

"Well, yeah—"

"So, tell me, just between you and me, what's the least-busy time of the day to visit his shop in West Shinjuku?"

"I guess I'll have to ask him next time I *see* him."

The nurse watched him walk toward the exits and permitted herself a disappointed sigh. Which may explain why she didn't catch the brief flash of a white dress out of the corner of her eye as it passed by her, and headed down the hallway leading deeper into the building.

The hospital had erupted into a quiet panic when the ambulance announced it was carrying Setsura Aki. Nobody wanted to treat him. No matter how skilled the doctor, all his shortcomings would be revealed once the patient was reexamined by Doctor Mephisto.

Simply imagining how the hospital director would deal with whoever presumed to treat this young owner of an old and established *senbei* shop—and the best P.I. in Shinjuku—was enough to make everybody from the assistant director on down think twice before volunteering his services.

Somehow, before the ambulance arrived, an attending physician was decided upon. Within twenty minutes the patient's condition was diagnosed as a "bioenergetic breakdown, cause unknown."

Two young women accompanied him. The shop girl was treated for a bout of lightheadedness and sent home. Takako Kanan remained with Setsura. She said she was a friend from outside Shinjuku, and the fact that she was the daughter of a renowned scholar convinced the doctors.

The array of bedside sensors relayed the patient's condition directly to the nurse's station and to the attending physician's office, so they saw no reason not to let her stay there. As a friend, she could prop up his spirits and provide moral support.

Takako sat on the sofa in the luxurious, two-room medical suite. The sofa was next to the bed where Setsura lay with his eyes closed. She tried not to stare at him too much. She got a paperback history text out of her purse. Scanning the tiny text and detailed illustrations, though, she became aware that her attention had been drawn once again to the white, exhausted face.

She shook her head in reproach and averted her gaze. As if waiting for this moment, a warm sensation flared up in her chest. This man had declared war on the monster from the shadow box in order to save her. And such courage came from a man lovelier than most women.

What she was feeling, she told herself, was gratitude. But she knew that the very first time they'd met at the bar on Fifth Street, this young man had left a searing brand upon her heart.

A movement out of the corner of her eye caught her attention. His arms lay on the blanket across his stomach. One hand twitched mysteriously. He'd fallen into a comatose state in the ambulance and remained dead to the world. Trying to imagine what force of the subconscious was prompting such behavior left her utterly vexed.

Takako didn't know that even in an unconscious state, the devil wires had flowed from his fingers, slipped through the jamb of the automatic doors, and had stretched a cordon around the entire floor.

At that same moment, something wicked this way

came, tearing through the invisible coils of razor wire, the hospital room in her sights.

Even in a coma, Setsura Aki would keep on fighting to the bitter end.

Feeling a cool breeze on the back of her neck, Takako jumped up and checked the window on the far side of the bed. Nothing there was out of the ordinary. She whirled around.

A woman in a white *cheongsam* stood in the doorway. Her hand covered half of her face. The other half—more beautiful than anything else in the universe—gazed down at Setsura.

"We meet at last," she said in an indescribable voice. "Yes, you are the man I saw that night. I have come to see you breathe your last."

Takako felt the silent air growing frigid around her. She frantically stifled the scream rising in her throat.

"Who—Who are you?"

It took a long second for the woman to register Takako's presence. She lowered her left hand. Takako's scream died in her lungs. The other half of the woman's incomparably beautiful face was a hideous mass of charred flesh.

To be continued.

Afterword

Demon City Shinjuku may well have met its most dangerous enemies ever.

Vampires.

These three (Kikiou is a different species of immortal) are not ordinary vampires. They are messengers of the night, thousands of years old and in possession of untold powers.

Even the combined forces of Setsura Aki and Doctor Mephisto may not be enough to resist them, as when Mephisto's fortress-like hospital is easily penetrated without the perpetrators breaking a sweat.

Creating a heroic, vampire-themed, supernatural battle has long been a dream of mine. I don't think a vampire story has been depicted in quite this way before. That's not the sole reason, but the originally planned two volumes have soared past a thousand pages.

Ideas bubbled out of my head one after the other, and I couldn't bring myself to discard any of them. The story has evolved enormously and the number of characters keeps growing. Keeping all those balls in the air from installment to installment is a big challenge.

But fear not.

Everything will be resolved in its own good time. The light at the end of the tunnel isn't an oncoming train. I'm not one for meaningless endings. The road ahead may look bleak, but you can trust me on this.

The one person qualified to challenge that claim is my editor, Mr. T. On occasion, a serialization scheduled to run a hundred and thirty pages has run into a brick wall after fifty or seventy. At times like that, Mr. T is wont to shout, "Man, I'm out of here!"

"Let's take that long walk off a short pier together then."

"Ah, this sofa is stained with the blood, sweat and tears of your poor editor," he blusters, in a mixture of intimidation and resignation.

But looking at him out of the corner of my eye, I catch a glittering premonition of developments that will far exceed anything we could expect or imagine if left to our own devices.

To start with, my dedication to the material is completely different. I really love my vampires. Even more than the infamous Miss Toya.

More than in any other previous work I've committed to novel form, I've been breathing new life into the old-school monsters you used to see in the movies, as the haunted atmosphere of *Demon City Shinjuku* turns into its own worst enemy.

This city exists if for no other reason than to tell the story of *Yashakiden.*

So to Mr. T and my readers I say, *relax.* I promise you that *Yashakiden* will succeed as a story unequaled in its class. Lost in the midst of the labyrinth, the mists of Transylvania swirling around me, I resolve to press forward, with hope and confidence as my sole sidearms.

But even when I put the final volume to bed, will that be the end of the tale?

Hideyuki Kikuchi (while watching *The Legend of the Seven Golden Vampires*)
May 28, 1989

May 2010

HIDEYUKI KIKUCHI

Creator of VAMPIRE HUNTER D,

Comes a dark world of demons, exorcists, and realities intertwining between the living... and the DEAD.

VOL. 1 manga
Available
DECEMBER
2009

ART:
SHIN YONG-GWAN

TAIMASHIN

THE RED SPIDER EXORCIST

退魔針 紅虫魔殺行

VOL. 1 ISBN: 978-1569670-134-8 $9.95

Taimashin 1: The Red Spider Exorcist - Taimashin 1 - First published in Japan in 2006 by MEDIA FACTORY, Inc.
English translation rights reserved by Digital Manga, Inc. Under license from MEDIA FACTORY, Inc., Tokyo.

evil remains... the saga continues

IDEYUKI KIKUCHI'S

Vampire Hunter D 3

ADAPTED AND ILLUSTRATED BY
SAIKO TAKAKI

AKA
AVAILABLE NOW!
AT AKADOT.COM

the manga based on the
3rd vampire hunter d novel,
ich sold over 30,000 units and inspired the hit film
vampire hunter d: Bloodlust!

uki kikuchi's vampire hunter d vol. 1	ISBN: 978-1-56970-827-9	$12.95
uki kikuchi's vampire hunter d vol. 2	ISBN: 978-1-56970-787-6	$12.95
uki kikuchi's vampire hunter d vol. 3	ISBN: 978-1-56970-788-3	$13.95

he official website:
ww.vampire-d.com

Kikuchi's VAMPIRE HUNTER D © 2009 Hideyuki Kikuchi/Digital Manga, Inc. All rights reserved.

NOW YOU CAN READ YOUR FAVORITE
DMP BOOKS ONLINE AT
emanga
eマンガ.COM
LET'S DRAW MANGA
ORIGINAL CONTENT
OUT OF PRINT TITLES
CHECK FREQUENTLY FOR SPECIAL PROMOTIONS!!
LOTS OF YAOI MANGA!
EXCLUSIVE ONLINE CONTENT
CHECK US OUT AT
EMANGA.COM
RED © Sanae Rokuya. All rights reserved. Original Japanese edition published in 2006 by Taiyoh Tosho Publishing Co., Ltd
NEW BEGINNINGS - HARETE BOKUTACHIWA © KOTETSUKO YAMAMOTO. All rights reserved. Original Japanese edition pu
by Taiyoh Tosho Publishing Co., Ltd. Cho Ni Naru Hi / The Day I Become a Butterfly © Sumomo Yumeka 2005. Originally pu
in 2005 by Taiyoh Tosho Co., Ltd. LOST BOYS © Kaname Itsuki 2004. Originally published in Japan in 2004 by Taiyoh
DOUSAIBOU SEIBUTSU / SAME CELL ORGANISM © Sumomo 2001. Originally published in Japan in 2001 by Taiyoh Tosho
Let's Draw Manga - Drawing Yaoi © 2007 by DIGITAL MANGA, Inc. All rights reserved.